A WOMAN CALL[ED EN]

■ **Tomie Ōhara** was born and brought up in a small mountainous village in Shikoku Island, in the western part of Japan. En to Iu Onna (*A Woman Called En*) first appeared in 1960, and it won two major literary awards. Tomie Ōhara is the author of a number of other novels, including *Onna wa Ikiru* (*A Woman Lives*), *Akumeitakaki Onna* (*Notorious Woman*), an autobiographical novel, *Nemuru Onna* (*Sleeping woman*), and *Chijo o Tabi Suru Mono* (*Journeying the Earth*) to be published by Pandora.

The translators met in London in 1979 when Kazuko Furuhata was living there for five years with her family. After translating *A Woman Called En*, Kazuko returned to Tokyo, where she is writing an account of her life in England. Janet Smith works as a social worker in London.

A WOMAN CALLED EN

'En to Iu Onna'

Tomie Ōhara

Translated by Kazuko Furuhata
and Janet Smith

PANDORA

Routledge & Kegan Paul
London and New York

This English translation
first published in 1986
Pandora Press (Routledge & Kegan Paul plc)
11 New Fetter Lane, London EC4P 4EE

Published in the USA by Routledge & Kegan Paul Inc.
in association with Methuen Inc.
29 West 35th Street, New York, NY 10001

Set in Sabon 10/13pt.
by Columns of Reading
and printed in Great Britain
by The Guernsey Press Co. Ltd.
Guernsey, Channel Islands.

Library of Congress Cataloging in Publication Data

Ōhara, Tomie, 1912–
A woman called En = En to iu onna.
Translation of: En to iu onna.
1. Nonake, En, 1660-1726—Fiction. I. Title.
II. Title: En to iu onna.
PL835.H3E513 1986 895.6'35 85-19430

British Library CIP data also available

ISBN 0-86358-079-3 (c)
0-86358-082-3 (pb)

CONTENTS

PREFACE
THE WOMAN WITHIN ME

Since my youth, Nonaka En and her remarkable life have held a place in my heart. I always wanted to write about her.

I knew of En from early childhood, having grown up in the area where she was born. When I was a schoolgirl. I became consumptive and was bedridden for several years. A long, solitary period in a sickbed is a life of confinement: my adolescence was just like En's. Later, when I started writing En, this experience was a clue to a clearer understanding of her life in exile. In fact, it came to me so intensly that I was able to write as if I myself were the heroine.

When I learnt, in 1942, that Kochi Prefectural Library held twenty or more of En's letters, the character was reborn in my mind and came to life once more. I was fortunate to be allowed to study the letters as they were preserved in a section of the library not open to the public. As I read them I was filled with emotion. I felt as if I were violating the privacy of her correspondence. They were all written with a strong brush stroke in fine, dark ink, on handmade paper and vividly and openly expressed her feelings. They were written after she returned from exile and were mostly addressed to Tani Shinzan. She wrote freely and honestly about how hard it was to exist in the outside world where she had, for the first time, come to live. She agonized over her situation and the fact that she could do nothing about it. The graphic and realistic manner in which her life was revealed in the letters made me feel as if En were speaking directly to me.

I accepted it as a testament from En that her letters had been made available to me, especially since, shortly afterwards, they were all destroyed in an air raid in 1945. After reading the letters I knew I had to write about this woman called En, not because I wanted to, but because it was my duty to do so. From that time on, the woman called En became the inspiration for my work. But it was not until much later that I accomplished my goal.

For like En, I too had to experience more than forty years of living before I could write about the woman who, at the age of forty-four, was pardoned and started her difficult and hopeless life. My life was severe, lonely and harsh then. En's experiences and mine were very similar. There are parallels, not only in the confinement of our youth, but also in the differences between a man and a woman in expressing love, in severe criticism of them and in the sadness and emptiness of unrequited love. I could not write En until I had matured and understood all of this. I believe the days of my youth are embodied and described in *A Woman Called En*.

I am delighted that the story has been translated into English and will be available to the English-speaking world. I am most grateful to the translators and to the Japan Foreign-Rights Centre.

Tomie ŌHara
10 June 1985
(translated by Kazuko Furuhata)

TRANSLATORS' NOTE

It is perhaps a paradox that the translation of this story of a woman alone was inspired by a friendship between two women. En's solitary struggle to create a meaningful independent life bore little relation to our sharing and mutual support. Yet in deciding to bring the work of an important Japanese woman writer to English speaking readers, we ultimately chose *A Woman Called En* because so many aspects of her story struck a chord in our present day experience.

Any translator must enjoy words and the process of language. The contrasts and similarities between two such totally different languages as Japanese and English are particularly interesting. In this novel Tomie Ōhara has used archaic, classical prose to recreate the atmosphere of seventeenth-century writing; it is a complex and at times lengthy style, difficult even for Japanese readers and often impossible to translate literally. Moreover, while the mood throughout the novel is restrained, the original language permits a richness of prose which could only be regarded as 'purple' in English.

It has been fascinating to observe how the structure of Japanese conveys psychological and cultural insights, for it is far more elaborate in the language of courtesy and respect than any European tongue. Not only the grammatical forms, but also the actual vocabulary, still depend upon the speaker and the deference accorded to the person addressed. In the rigidly hierarchical society of the Edo Period these forms were extremely complex and in particular the language of women was at all times more polite than that of men. Some of this, if translated, becomes absurd, as in 'my superior father' or 'honourable letter'. However, although there are several words for 'kneel' for instance, a knowledge of the different types of kneeling which relate to the degree of respect paid to one's companion enables this concept to be accurately expressed in English.

The author's considerable knowledge of Japanese history, of classical poetry and Chinese literature is reflected in her writing. Because she assumes the reader's awareness of such things, we felt a need and found pleasure in researching them for ourselves. We delved into the politics and the economy of the Edo Period, into education and into medieval Neo-Confucianist philosophy, and we looked at the structure of traditional Japanese poetry. Yet we found that very little had been written about the lives and status of women in the seventeenth century. It is therefore all the more remarkable that Tomie Ōhara has created such a full and solid characterization of En. She came alive for us and although we re-read and re-translated many times, we remained moved by her predicament.

Finally, we would like to take this opportunity of thanking Dr I.J. McMullen for translating *Chuyoshoku: Commentary on the Doctrine of the Golden Mean*. We are very grateful for his assistance.

Kazuko Furuhata
Janet Smith

INTRODUCTION

JAPANESE SOCIETY IN THE SEVENTEENTH CENTURY

This tale is the fictionalized biography of a lady, known in her lifetime as an eccentric, beautiful woman of strong will. She passed into local history and folklore, renowned for her determined independence in an age when women were totally subordinate to men. The author grew up in the castle town of Kōchi where the heroine was born and thus knew of her from early childhood. All the characters mentioned were real people, and gravestones or memorials for many of them are still standing.

The story also reflects many aspects of life in seventeenth-century Japan. In the early Edo Period (1600–1868) Japan was a feudal society, only recently unified and ruled by a military leader, the shōgun, from the Tokugawa clan, whose aim was to consolidate his clan's power after a hundred years of internal strife. By the second half of the century the renewed stability of the country had allowed for economic expansion and for a renaissance in arts and learning. There was a price to pay, in the strict control and many restrictive laws, but in a country where absolute and unquestioning loyalty to one's master was the supreme virtue, such control was readily enforceable.

The control of land was vital because at this time all wealth and payments were measured in rice yield or koku (one koku was about five bushels or 180 litres). The shogun and his vassal lords held about 60 per cent of the land, in the most strategic positions – encircling the capital, Edo, and controlling transport routes and areas of doubtful loyalty. This enabled the Government to centralize the country's administration and to supervise the daimyō, the lords. Over a period of fifty years many laws were promulgated to fulfil this last aim.

One of the most onerous was the system of Alternate-Attendance, originally a voluntary show of allegiance, but made law in 1635. A lord and his retinue were required to spend six months of every year at the shōgun's court in Edo. Moreover, when the lord returned to his estate, his wife and children had to remain in the capital as hostages. This ensured the lord's loyalty but continually drained his finances and divided his power base so that he could not rebel. Castle building was also seen as potentially rebellious, implying as it did preparation for attack and the raising of an army, so decrees were issued limiting castles to one per province. Even repairs needed official sanction. There were also severe restrictions on all travel, with government control of all roads and ports and permission required before a journey could be undertaken. The government was thus able, in theory, to monitor all movement throughout the country, although this resulted in the already slow transport being further delayed by bureaucracy.

There were four social classes, rigidly stratified in an edict of 1586; samurai, farmers, artisans and merchants. In a population of between twenty-five to thirty million, there were about two million samurai, the only group permitted to bear arms. However, by the mid-seventeenth century most were town-dwellers and administrators for their clan lord. Further, as the Tokugawa shōguns abolished fiefs and confiscated land from time to time, numbers of masterless samurai were created, many of whom were perceived as troublemakers, and who certainly took some time to be absorbed into the general population. The farmer's chief duty was to raise tax for his lord and he had few, if any, rights, not even the right to a family name. The merchants were considered the lowest class because they held no land. However they were often extremely rich and became important arbiters of taste in city life. Membership of each class was hereditary. The prevailing Neo-Confucianist philosophy was used to reinforce the divisions by emphasis on loyalty to one's lord. In any event such loyalty was seen to be an indissoluble bond, lasting through generations. In this context, if one member of a family fell from favour, it was quite logical and usual for the whole family to be placed under house arrest until the male line had died out. Sons were expected to avenge their father, given the chance.

The stabilization of the country freed manpower for the expansion of industry and agriculture. As a lord's rice yield proclaimed his wealth and status, the use of as much land as possible was encouraged. Land reclamation, a developing science for over 150 years, reached a peak and, with new skills in river control and irrigation engineering, the amount of useable land had doubled by the end of the seventeenth century.

In foreign policy Japan had held an ambivalent relationship with China from earliest times, trading, sending ambassadors and planning invasion. Europeans first came to Japan from Portugal, as traders and missionaries, in 1549, with the Spanish, Dutch and English coming close upon each other's heels fifty to sixty years later. Although initially in favour of the visitors because they had easier access to trade with China and because they brought the new military technology of firearms, the shōguns eventually found that the advent of

Christianity introduced deep religious rivalries. The quarrelling between Portuguese Jesuits and Spanish Franciscans, between Catholic and Protestant, was too threatening at a time when Japan had only recently brought its warlike Buddhist monks to order. The Europeans were seen as undermining the new stability of the country while in the free ports the feudal lords were seen to benefit at the expense of the shōgun. The number of anti-Christian edicts were thus a direct response to these two threats. Although the laws were not strictly enforced initially, after 1611 a long period of harsh persecution began. This culminated in the permanent expulsion of all Europeans by 1640 (apart from a minimal toleration of the Dutch), and in all Japanese being forbidden even to travel abroad. Thus the country was closed completely, to further reinforce Tokugawa power.

The influence of China, however, remained, in philosophy and culture. When the first Tokugawa Shōgun came to power the majority of the people was still illiterate, but as education received official patronage two aspects of scholarship developed. Chinese remained the language of wisdom and reading, while Japanese was used for writing, but was considered as a more feminine, and therefore an inferior, art. Commentaries on the great classical Chinese works of Confucius and Mencius were produced, and older commentaries reprinted. By far the most important of these were the works of the twelfth century Neo-Confucianist scholar Chu Hsi. His discourses outlined the duties of subjects and rulers in a rational and humanistic way and as such were readily adaptable to political administration, as well as providing an added justification for the rigid social order.

In keeping with their low status, the education of women was rare, apart from moral instruction on obedience and domestic preparation for marriage. Some samurai women were educated at home but were expected to study the Japanese classics and cultivate literary skill and refinement. They were also advised to keep their knowledge secret, lest men be jealous. As a mark of adulthood, aristocratic girls blackened their teeth and shaved their eyebrows. Lower-class women waited until marriage. All women were expected to marry, for political or dynastic considerations if samurai or noble. A woman who remained single was very rare and considered a disgrace to her family. Women could be divorced for domestic incompetence or for failure to produce a son and, although men could take any number of wives or concubines, the penalty for female adultery was death. The slightest hint of impropriety was an enormous disgrace to a woman, her family and her lords; any friendship with a man was considered immoral and even to be alone with a man was shameful.

Such is the social and political background to the events portrayed in Ōhara's novel. She depicts most vividly the intellectual climate and the effects of repression in her tale of the fate of this one family living in seventeenth-century Japan.

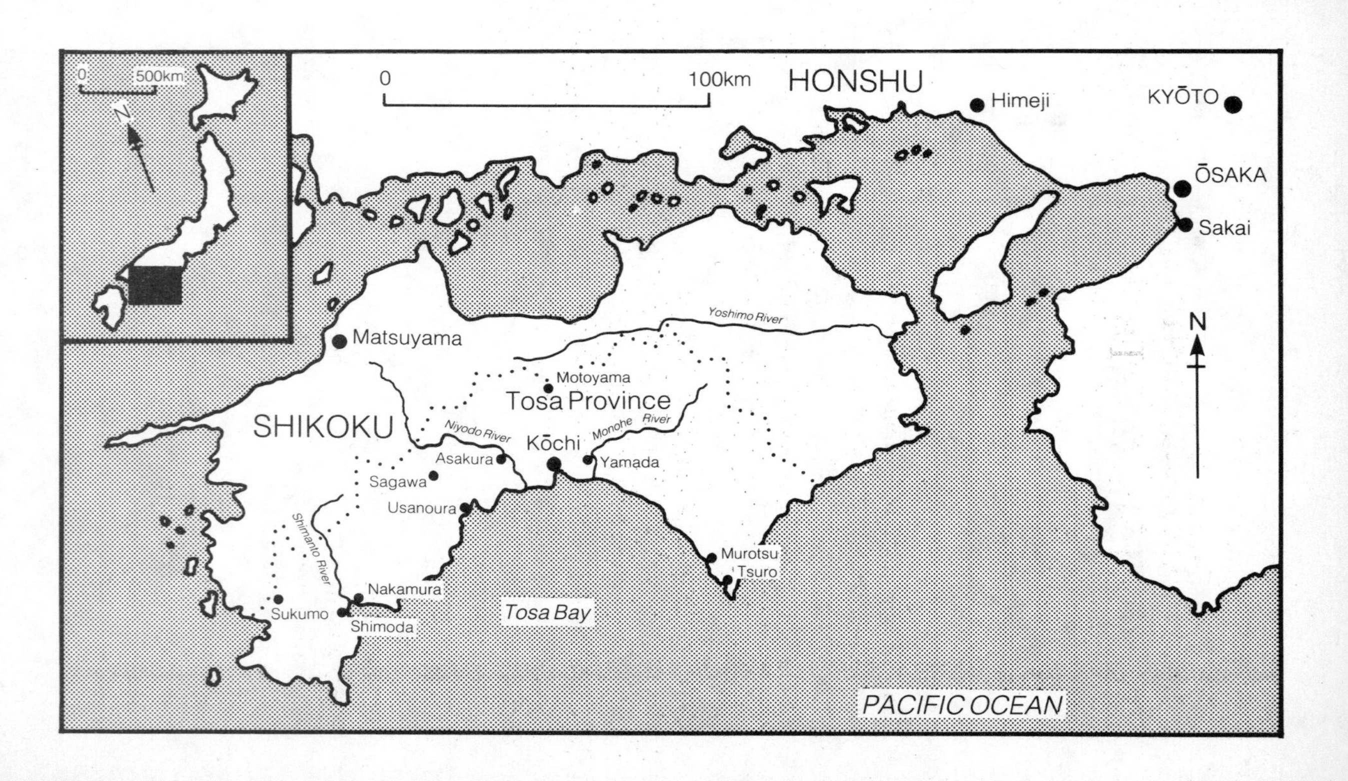

Southern Japan: Shikoku and part of Honshu

– 1 –

CONCERNING THE PARDON

A messenger from the Andō family came today, bearing our pardon from the clan government.

After he had gone, we all wept together, my nurse, my elder and younger sister and I, with mother in the middle.

'Why must I cry? I don't feel like crying.' Yet despite these thoughts, the tears were flowing freely.

Although we were all weeping and clinging to each other in this manner (mother was eighty, nurse sixty-five, my sisters and I over forty) the tears held a different emotion for me.

'How wonderful, congratulations,' we were saying to each other as we wept, but although I too congratulated my dear mother, it did not accord with my feelings.

Since our youngest brother Teishirō had died on 29 June, ten weeks ago, everyone had been eagerly anticipating this day. I, more than the others, was especially looking forward to it with a full heart, believing that after his death a pardon would be granted.

Teishirō's illness had worsened, and he himself knew that we could not expect him to recover.

'When I die, they will pardon you, dear sisters. That seems the best thing I can do for you all,' he said.

'What are you saying?' I remonstrated. 'What would the pardon mean to us after all this time? We have all grown old here, mother, sisters and I. Any change would bring misfortune. We shall be happy if we can live as we are; for like this, nothing changes, nothing happens. We should all be alive together. You must get better and live for us. That will make us happy.'

I really believed so. 'I shall remain in this house where we have lived under arrest for forty years,' I thought. 'When I am fifty, and sixty, I shall still live here. And even when I am seventy years old, and when I reach eighty like mother, I shall continue living here.'

Yet in the midst of relief and amusement I was aware of the bitter irony against myself. 'Nonaka En, detained at the age of four, put herself here for ninety years.'

If I were permitted to inscribe on my own tombstone. I would wish it to be written thus, not as 'lived here', but 'put herself here', because I had not really lived.

I did not want him to die. I profoundly wished that my brother would not die. He had been carried into this house by a nurse when he was but five months old, and now he was a forty-year-old man, lying on his deathbed.

Our family had been put in here for forty years and prohibited from taking even one step out of doors, prohibited from marriage and forbidden any contact with the outside world. None of us, brothers or sisters, really lived; we were just put.

Having been brought into this house at the age of four, I had no knowledge of life, nor had my younger brother and sister. But death called, just as surely, on those in prison, whether or not they knew what it was to live.

It was clear that my brother was going to die. We knew quite well that death was approaching.

Several of my brothers and sisters had died during those forty years. Death had visited them here in turn, starting with those who had most experience of living.

My eldest sister was eighteen years old. Two years

before our arrest, she had married one of the clan retainers and borne a child but she was separated from her husband and child and put away with us, as our father's blood ran in her veins.

She was the only one of whom we could say that she had actually lived. And death called on her first.

She survived barely three years here. Because she knew already what life meant, she could not survive more than three years.

Twelve years after this, my eldest brother died at thirty-one, followed by my second brother four years later. Fifteen years went by, then the third brother, whom I loved dearly, was gone.

Teishirō was now the only man in our Nonaka family and he was going to die.

Although I did not wish it, I was sure he would die. I had seen much death in this house. I knew what death looked like.

I felt like suffocating at the thought of Teishirō having only five months of freedom until his death at forty-one.

But when mother said that his death put an end to the Nonaka line, that it was not worth living, and asked us to die together, I shrank with fear.

I made up my mind to live on, until eighty or even ninety.

I had to use persuasive words to soothe her so that she would not kill herself.

'If we all commit suicide now, nobody will be able to bury him. Nor will there be any way to comfort the souls of father and our brothers who died one after another. We have to live and wait for the pardon and then set up a house for the dead Nonakas,' I urged.

While I was persuading her, I realized that I believed the pardon would come and that I was eagerly awaiting it.

'After we are released and step into a new world, I can

really start to live.' I felt myself becoming excited.

The next two months or so were very hard. My mind was more tense now in anticipation of the pardon than at any time in all the last forty years.

My two surviving half-sisters, unlike me, were not expecting the pardon. Rather, they thought it would be a burden. They said, 'Even if we are set free, what can we do after such a long time? It will only turn us adrift. We prefer to end our lives here.'

I felt uneasy and fearful, of course, about a new, unseen world, but my sisters had finished living already, without having experienced life at all.

'I am not like they are. I am now going to live for the first time in my life. After I receive the pardon, I shall go back to the castle town of Kōchi, and see *that gentleman*.'

My heart and soul were quivering, but I concealed it most carefully from my sisters. Although I believed it inwardly, nobody could really know whether or not we would be granted a pardon.

The pardon has come at last!

Everybody was excited. Even my two sisters, who had not looked forward to it and had imagined it almost as a burden, were shaken.

We offered a light to the souls of our brothers who had died while under arrest, and talked until morning. The five of us, two very old ones, and three not so young women, all wept and talked until we were exhausted and towards dawn, we dispersed into two rooms and went to bed.

Soon mother fell asleep, worn out. Her soft, heavy breathing was like the sound of a broken reed.

In the darkness, a faint smile played about my lips.

At last we had the pardon.

My father had been a harsh realist. Throughout his brief life he had passionately pursued his political aims.

His enemies' enduring, merciless hatred had run its course and I wondered if it had now softened a fraction towards his family.

No. For them, the pardon did not change their hatred. There was no drop of sentimentality there.

They assumed that the Nonaka line had ended when all the men in the family had died. Even though the family had three sisters over forty, none would be likely to conceive a child. Even if they could, the woman is only a vessel. All depends upon fathers. For this reason, my sister's baby daughter had been allowed to stay free at her father's house.

To them, it had simply become pointless to continue guarding women prisoners.

It would be proper to say that we were not counted as human. A cynical smile played about my lips.

No matter. I am not interested in politics or power. I want to live very much, but just quietly in a corner. Somehow or other I want to live.

You have nothing to fear. I am merely a woman of forty, and even if I live for all I am worth, what can you possibly be frightened of?

O Teishirō and my three poor brothers, being men, you could never be released. No pardon would be granted as long as you lived, even if you had reached fifty or sixty.

Being men, you had to die so that you could bring me alive.

See how I, a woman, can live more easily. Although I cannot imagine how a forty-year-old woman will cope, I shall try to survive.

I yearned for my eldest half-sister who had died young. Although I cannot recall her face easily, I think she was a quiet, fair-skinned woman. I was small and she gave me the impression of being very quiet, burdened as she was by her misfortune, but I am not sure now.

I have just one vivid memory of her. It is about her breasts. . . .

In the shadow of the paper sliding door between the kitchen and the nurses's room, she was kneeling forward, extracting the milk from them. It must have been quite soon after we were arrested, for she was still tortured by swollen breasts.

A white cup was placed in front of her on the wooden floor, she bent her head and squeezed out the milk. It gushed forth and was collected in the cup.

They seemed very strange to me, those breasts – tight, heavy and engorged, and with red veins visible on the pale pink flesh. On her white, pitifully thin chest they appeared to have a life of their own. They seemed on the one hand to be like fragrant, beautiful flowers and on the other to be possessed by a dreadfully deformed monster.

They were not at all like those of my mother, who was then already over forty. She had withered, pendulous breasts with pale blue veins on them.

While I was unwittingly watching, with these confused feelings, by chance she missed the cup and the white milk spurted out onto my face, right into my eyes. I cried loudly. When, soothed by the nurses, I stopped crying only to find her weeping, I felt embarrassed, as if I had caused her tears.

Ten years later, when I grew to womanhood, I remembered her strangely swollen breasts as 'living'.

Those breasts knew what 'living' was. Those pale pink breasts with red veins seemed to be simultaneously like freshly opened, mysterious flowers and like ghastly moving creatures.

It was those breasts which kept her alive for three years after her arrest and it was those breasts which made her unable to bear life beyond that time.

Had they comforted her she might have tried to live.

But her breasts, like a monster, must have tortured her pitiful thin body and tormented her soul, day and night.

Now in my fancy I can see a man's hands on her freshly blooming breasts, loving and caressing them. I can imagine the palms of a man's hands caressing her breasts to make them mysteriously grow and bloom.

When I neared her age and my breasts began to swell, I was terrified to think that they would grow into such swollen, sinister creatures. I bound my chest tightly so that the swellings would not show.

Yet though I did not know why, I already knew that I must not permit my breasts to become sinister, swollen creatures and must not let them blossom like some rich mysterious flower.

I was fearful, for I detected something like a sense of sin on my body.

When I was with my brothers, I felt a desire to hide not only my breasts but also my waist, my arms and legs, my cheeks and neck, to keep every part of my maturing body from their sight.

In truth it felt like a sin for me to be maturing as a woman.

Here in this house, time should have stood still. We should all have remained just as when we were put here.

(. . . Alas, poor Kinroku who died mad. . . .)

The house was too small for me to feel comfortable and I shut myself in my room. I was most reluctant even to go out into the garden.

I saw my carefree elder sister look after our brothers diligently, but I also minded and was deeply embarrassed by her. With a book open, I would sit gloomily in front of the desk, my whole body feeling feverish and heavy.

But in front of my brothers, I tried to conceal my thoughts. If they had realized my conflict, it would have insulted them and I would have been utterly mortified.

My dead older sister had been womanly and lovely. Although I had reached her age, I wondered why I felt stained with sin.

She was a woman who had bloomed naturally. By contrast, I did not blossom outwardly but turned inward to become stagnant and unbearably foul and diseased. I felt weak and felt that the odour of sin emanated from me.

Sitting with my brothers, it was agony for me to listen to Seishichi giving us lessons on Chu Hsi's *Elementary Learning* and on *Commentary on the Four Books*.[1]

For about ten years, between my sister's death and my eldest brother's death, it was sufficiently quiet and peaceful for me to find some happiness.

Seishichi, my eldest brother, was sixteen, Kinroku was fifteen, and my third brother Kishirō was eight when we were taken into this house with my elder sister Kanjo, my younger sister Shōjo and the youngest brother Teishirō. Gradually over the years each of my seven sisters and brothers came to a realization of their condition.

My mother and the other mothers, whose children were my half brothers and sisters, were officially my father's servants. Although the nurses were not included as prisoners, they followed us willingly. And in fact all of us, mothers and children, spent the days quite contentedly.

Compared with 10,000 Koku[2] which we had received when our father was alive, we now received only seventy Koku. Although we were prohibited from taking even one step out of the gate to see other people, this was my world until I reached the age of discretion. For me this house was not small. I was free enough.

Only when my body began to mature and I experienced

that sense of shame and I felt I was exposing myself to the eyes of my elder brothers, did this house become too small for me to feel free.

A bamboo palisade, with its tall, sharply-cut ends pointing to the sky, surrounded this lone house in the mountains, and there were always soldiers in the guard house. I knew that outside the palisade there was a world where men had their liberty.

So the sense of shame and the premonition of misfortune which I experienced as my body matured began to come true. From about that time there were signs of ill-luck in my family.

At the end of the year, when I was seventeen, my eldest brother Seishichi grew weak and on 13 June in the summer of 1679, when I was nineteen, he passed away. He was thirty-one years old.

When he was young, he had been taken to Edo as a hostage and brought up there to ensure family obedience to the government. In July 1663 when my father lost his position and went into retirement, my brother Seishichi was summoned home and became head of the household. And the next year, on 3 March, my family was placed under arrest and was ordered into exile.

In this house, my brother suffered for fifteen years before he died. He knew he would not be released as long as he lived.

He had gained some, albeit inadequate, idea of life and he knew he had to survive in here.

He was determined to teach us, his younger brothers and sisters, about life. What little we knew of human living during that forty years was wholly thanks to him. It was due to the seed of learning which he sowed in our hearts while he was alive.

He taught us to read and write. I gained great enjoyment from books. Living is reading a book and understanding it. That is everything, I thought, and was content.

During that time, the house was peaceful and my eldest brother was healthy. But when he became ill and bedridden, I realized that book learning was not life. I began to understand what the last ten years or so had meant to him.

I sensed how pitiful and miserable he was in bed. On the one hand I wanted to sympathize with him and console him, but on the other hand a hardness of heart grew inside me.

Initially this cruelty sprouted against Seishichi, later against the other brothers who were to die: against poor Kinroku who died mad, against my third brother Kishirō whom I respected most and against my beloved younger brother Teishirō whose death moved me to many tears. As my brothers died one after the other, it stayed quietly in the depths of my soul, gleaming dimly like a sword in a marsh.

What was this terrible feeling I had against my brothers who died in vain one after another?

I understand it a little now. It was because I was a woman, and we were brothers and sisters.

Men and women of the same family . . . I found it such a frustrating relationship. Those chains of inhibition were so strong and yet so futile.

The abiding sense of sin, which forced me desperately to try to hide my swelling breasts, and the strong, irrational, cruel feeling developed solely because we were brothers and sisters.

We had such a hopelessly sad relationship.

We lived in harmony with each other and I loved my elder brothers just as they loved me. Yet, just as I secretly felt hard-hearted, I am sure they too unconsciously felt cruel towards us.

Perhaps they dreamed of cruelly and shamelessly

violating me and my sisters.

(. . . I can still hear Kinroku's dreadful scream in the room where he was caged.)

Besides such hard-heartedness against my eldest brother Seishichi, I also experienced a kind of resentment. I felt that, for some obscure reason, I had been deceived by him. My growing body taunted me, showed me that knowledge was not life and made me feel spiteful towards my brother.

What end could learning serve? For us, confined here for our lifetime, what could the teachings of Confucius, Mencius and Chu Hsi show? Being confined here till death, how could we make use of the paths of virtue and the words of sages, without seeing, loving, or talking to anyone?

I knew myself how shameful it would be to speak of my resentment. Because of that it boiled up inside me all the more.

It seemed as if he were lying to me. It was infuriating for me to look at my quiet, gentle eldest brother. On the one hand I loved and respected him like my own father but on the other I wished I could humiliate him and I wanted to show him up in his true colours.

I also began secretly to reject the many teachings which I had originally absorbed and understood with excitement.

We prisoners could only find it all meaningless. I begrudged my former enthusiasm for such meaningless things, feeling I had been deceived by my eldest brother's fluent speech.

But I would not have resented him for such a thing, if we had not been brother and sister. It can surely be said that the decision by my father's political opponents to punish us as a family for forty years, completely achieved its aim. My father's eight children were punished by their family ties two or three times more than intended.

As head of the kin, as the present head of the Nonaka family in exile, my eldest brother was always quietly reading; he taught us as a father as well as a teacher, and silently accepted until the day he died the irrational resentment and cruelty which remained deep in my heart.

I did not believe he would die. I was profoundly shocked. Because I had never imagined he would die, I had allowed resentment and cruelty to spring up inside me.

Twelve years had passed since my eldest sister died.

Seishichi had retained the aura of the outer world, the world of men, where he had lived until he was sixteen. There was about him something of the city life of Edo. From his demeanour and his words I sometimes caught a fleeting glimpse of the outer world which I had never seen, and the aura of a man's world. Plainly this tempted me.

From childhood, I had always loved, respected and obeyed him. Yet when I became a woman I resented him deeply. When he died, I recognized that both emotions had something to do with my eagerness for the human world, gleaned from him, and the impossibility of attaining it.

Four years passed. In 1683 my second brother, Kinroku, died mad.

Kinroku, my half-brother, one year younger than the dead Seishichi, had always lived beside him like a shadow.

After our eldest brother died, Kinroku became uncommunicative. He was always silent, as if he were listening to a creature inside himself.

What creature could it be? We did not much question his silence, as he had always been taciturn and we were overcome with sorrow over the death of our eldest brother. We were oppressed by constant recollections of him and filled with dejection about the future. We were preoccupied with our own burdens.

Nobody could know the shape or type of creature in Kinroku's heart, which bit into his flesh and sucked his blood to live. We made no attempt to know.

The monster consumed his heart, sucked all his blood and took over his body. Then one morning, all of a sudden, it changed into him and leapt out. Until then, we had been so careless that we had no idea what sort of monster tormented him or how difficult it had been for this silent man who had shut himself in his room.

Our thoughtlessness permitted poor Kinroku to fall a victim to the monster. With an inner cry, my poor elder brother must have been begging us for help.

His piteous shriek reaches my ears now.

If my family had not left him alone and if we had not allowed him to shut himself quietly in his room, Kinroku might not have collapsed into a wretched death from madness. We should have made it clear to him that we were depending on him to be a pillar of strength and head of the Nonaka family after we lost our eldest brother.

I wish we could have made him realize that he was indispensable.

I understand it now. He was initially possessed, driven to madness and tortured till his death, not by his love for the dead Seishichi, but by his own weakness, his sense of inferiority and his powerlessness.

After the death of our eldest brother, Kinroku, now head of the unfortunate Nonaka family, had received a notice from the clan government stating that our allowance was reduced by almost half, from a ration for seventy persons to that for thirty-six persons.

Notification
From 1 July
Following the death of Nonaka Seishichi in June,
A ration for thirty-six persons will be granted to Nonaka Kinroku and his brothers.
Details:
A ration for twenty-one persons for three men
A ration for fifteen persons for three women
29 September 1679

This had pierced Kinroku's heart. The notice of reduced payment by the clan government was, he thought, an assessment against him, when compared with his elder brother. As he had always believed himself to be worthless, he accepted the notice as clearly demonstrating this.

However he should have understood how deeply the clan Government hated the survivors of the Nonaka family and the blood of my father.

Since Kinroku had grown up as a shadow of our eldest brother, I am sure he acquired the habit of thinking himself worthless. Moreover, there may have been an unwitting tendency in the family to take him lightly.

I never saw him set himself against our eldest brother or quarrel with him at all.

Only once, I remember an occasion when those two brothers were grappling like crazy men. They were wrestling with all their strength, each trying to overpower the other, and trying to get the other down.

My sister and I, on the verandah of the sitting room, ran up and down crying, 'Elder brothers, stop it please! Stop it please!'

To think that one of them might kill the other at any moment made me feel half dead with fright.

'O-En-sama, that's called Sumo. It's a brave sport for gentlemen. Do not fear.'

Although my nurse told me this repeatedly, my sister and I could not stop crying.

They were still madly jostling and violently grappling with each other. It was man's play, that murderous grappling and struggling, and only in that moment could my brothers be real men. The power which made them grapple was the embodiment of manhood. Only now do I understand, that was what made them challenge each other like madmen.

We could not believe our eyes. To be a man made us so frightened. However if we, as already adult sisters, had tried to be feminine, our elder brothers would probably have averted their eyes from such pointless vanity.

I had known it all the time. Just as they did not live as men, we, their sisters, did not live as women.

Like a group of strange sexless people, we brothers and sisters lived a lie.

It is said that an earthquake erupts out of the most fragile point of the earth's crust. In the same way the emptiness of such a false life may have found a fissure in Kinroku's sick heart and erupted out.

One morning Kinroku turned into a wild beast, sprang out and with terrible strength pinioned Kanjo, his younger sister, and held her down. On hearing our elder sister, Shōjo, scream, we ran up to them. We could hardly bear to look. We held our breath.

I was convinced that we brothers and sisters, punished because of the blood of our father, were at that moment absolutely punished to the full.

The Andō ordered a cage to be set up in a small room at the rear of the house. In this double prison, Kinroku was confined. He slept as if dead for a number of days; another day he started shouting something unintelligible in such a loud voice that it almost shook the house. At times he seemed frightened of something. He would weep loudly, or roar like a beast, so obscenely that I felt like covering my ears. Another day he suffered intense agony, bewailed his misfortune and asked us for help, or begged somebody's pardon.

Sometimes he seemed very happy, laughing merrily and dancing about. And sometimes he sat upright and still, with bony thin shoulders, as if he had become sane again.

Only Kinroku was free now. Here in this house, where order was narrowly kept by tolerating a lie, only Kinroku could speak, cry, laugh and bawl as much as he wanted. We pretended to be indifferent to it all, as if none of it could penetrate our eyes or ears. We had to do so.

I sat beside Teishirō, facing my elder, third brother Kishirō, with a desk between us, and I learned *Chuyoshoku* from him, with Kinroku's disgraceful howling in the background.

> The source of the Way proceeds from Heaven; its substance is endowed in the self; and may not be left for an instant. For this reason the superior man is watchful over himself, when he is alone.
>
> The Way is not far from men: to correct oneself and not to require much of others, to exercise the principle of reciprocity – this is not far at variance from the Way.
>
> Just as, for example, when one goes on a distant journey one begins close at hand, so the Way of the superior man finds its beginning close at hand in the relationship between man and wife, but at its utmost reaches, it shines brightly through heaven and earth.[4]

Even as I was listening to Kishirō's detailed lecture, little by little something insubordinate was growing in my heart.

(What a strange animal man is! Perhaps only politics has the power to excite such enthusiasm in men – like my father, like those who hated my father and punished us, and like the Sung and Tang emperors.)

I could not persuade myself to learn with my former sincerity. To put it another way, such moral teachings cavil at man's weakness. Now I wished to become acquainted with men, rather than simply listen to all that book learning.

I was aware that many people were making their lives far beyond this house; loving and hating, being jealous, deceiving and being betrayed. I desired to know at least one of them. I desperately wished to acquaint myself with at least one of them.

Kishirō had already noticed that my heart was not in the lessons and that I was yearning for something quite different.

'En, you seem to have grown tired of the lessons,' he said.

I did not miss this chance. I felt a strong desire to reveal to him the stagnation in my heart and I could feel the ill-will emerging.

'Since you have noticed, I am weary of the people depicted in those books. I would like to see a real live human being, just once.'

Kinroku had been quiet the last few days. He sat upright in the cage, like a sane man, and meditated, forlornly straightening his bony shoulders. Kanjo and Sōjo were preparing the evening meal and only the quiet clinking noises of the dishes reached our ears.

Kishirō was sitting uncomfortably on the narrow verandah, clasping his knees with his arms and looking up at the evening sky over the mountains, visible between the eaves and the high palisade.

'But En, it's enough to know one person after all, isn't it? I think so. Although it's a sort of prison here, we are not alone. We had our eldest brother and sister and we still have brothers and sisters as well as our mothers, haven't we?'

'You are right, dear brother, but in here. . . .' I wanted

to tell him, 'There is no unrelated person here. I need someone who is not a relative, one who has no blood relationship and who feels clean and cool', but of course I could not.

I could not say that without referring to my secret disgrace. It had something to do with my resentment that my elder brother was related to me; he was, in a word, forbidden, because we were brother and sister.

I was so embarrassed that I found I had answered unintentionally, '. . . I feel I would like to know about politics.'

Politics – a strange world where a man may ignore everything else. My father passionately lived for it and dared to incur this deep hatred which extended far into his children's lives; that unaccountable world where the Tang, Sung and Han emperors recklessly massacred and poisoned, till eventually they themselves were killed and died out.

My brother had recommended some books to me and told me, 'Without murder there's no history,' but I think that there's no history without hatred.

'To tell the truth, I would like to know what sort of person our father was. Where on earth did all this hatred spring from, this hatred which affects even us? I would like to understand the world of politics which brought it forth.'

I had listened to Seishichi, my mother and my nurse tell me many things about my father. He was a spirited, intelligent man, passionate in his pursuit of an ideal. After learning much of the doctrine of Zen, he then learned Confucianism, sitting late into the night for the lectures. He obtained an original text which had neither notes nor an explanatory Kana[5] ending, which he himself tried hard to annotate.

He succeeded to his foster father at the very early age of

twenty-two as an administrator of 240,000 Koku for the Tosa clan, and for twenty-seven years until his death, he put into practice in politics all his ideals and all the knowledge which he had learnt.

He cut through mountains to change the course of rivers, he built canals, cleared the land for farms and deepened ports for the use of large ships. His executive ability produced such fine results that it was said that there was no land, mountain or coast which remained uncultivated by my father's ideal hoe.

When I was a child, many of the stories about his life impressed and amused me very much. Gradually I came to idealize him as a man of great intelligence and an administrator of rare ability. I still feel happy to think of him as a remarkable, distinguished man.

I had another reason for this secret ill-feeling towards my elder brothers who died here in vain – they had neither my father's rare ability nor his great success.

I wonder if a woman is more likely to feel love, esteem and adoration for a strong man and ill-will towards a weak man. Although I knew quite well that my elder brothers' powerlessness was not their responsibility, I could not erase my hard-heartedness.

But it now occurs to me that this deep-rooted hatred against my father, which still affects us, may bear some relationship to my father himself.

'Although I think he was broken easily in his last years, dear brother, I am sure he was a remarkable man. For even after his death we are still so hated by his enemies. How did this hatred occur while he was still alive? I do want to know.'

He was silent for a while.

'I don't want to judge him. A woman has a shallow mind. You might not understand me. Being the son of such a great man, I do not regret finishing my life in here. Our elder brother also told me so when he was alive. In those days I disagreed with him. But now I understand him. Greatness is cruel and always demands a sacrifice. I hear our father used to read *Encountering Sorrow* by Ch'u Yüan[6] over and over in his last years when he retired to Nakano, after he lost his position.

> I bend my will and control myself.
> If I am judged to be guilty, I do not argue but listen stoically.
> Even if disgraced, I shall accept it, although I am blameless.
> Holy sages spoke of the virtue of being upright until death.

'. . . I accept it as my destiny. That is not resignation. I accept it positively. Here we may not have freedom of our bodies, but our spirits are free.

'Here we have the spiritual freedom to live as humans. It is a fact of politics that we live here under arrest. Nevertheless we feel affection and passion. (He glanced behind to where Kinroku was confined.) So we can say this is a small part of the real world. We can still call it the world of men.

'Even if we were to live outside, the world of men would be as small as our world here. It is as small as this anywhere.

'En, what do you think of a man who renounces society and enters the priesthood, who goes into a world where he has no freedom?'

'Perhaps . . .' I thought a while and answered, 'To him it is a world where he can live more freely and he might regard this as the best possible way to live. The state of the world where one can live in freedom would be different for each person. But I would like to have that gloomy world which those priests renounce. I would like to be given the chance to live there.'

Then I felt like making him laugh by reminding him of Sei Shōnagon's words that a Buddhist priest is as unimportant as a piece of wood.[7]

Or, as Kishirō said that a woman has a shallow mind, I wanted to say that a man is like a bottomless pit, so deep that he can't see anything.

(Since childhood I had been able to make all my family laugh in this manner. It might be the reason that my eldest brother, after he became bedridden, said he was always happy if I was beside him. He used to say that my liveliness made him feel more cheerful. While outwardly I pretended to be so lively, inwardly I did not know what to do with my shame-covered body, and I spent the days in such misery. In that way I was cheating him. I was keeping all that spite and cruelty deep in my heart. If he had looked right into my heart he would have said that woman was a deceiving creature.)

I knew then that we were not allowed to judge our father here, not because it would be undutiful, but because to doubt his politics and his greatness would shatter the meaning of our twenty years as prisoners.

It would be tragic if we, who spent all our lives as prisoners because of this, doubted his greatness.

It seemed that Kishirō thought he should not allow his brothers and sisters to feel such desolation, from which only death could bring release.

It seemed he made up his mind to accord the greatest respect to the memory of our father. Although I knew I was arrogant to question this memory, I pretended innocence in doing so.

He was intelligent and a profound thinker. I was almost

in love with him. I knew that he loved me too. In our hearts, we sometimes forgot we were brother and sister, and came close together in our love for each other.

But apart from that, I remember poor Kinroku rather than Kishirō, as a more familiar and friendly person; Kinroku who died mad, who behaved so violently and screamed out words so obscene that I wanted to cover my ears.

When sane, he was a man in whom I had no interest at all, in fact I regarded him unconsciously with contempt. But now his madness made him more likeable to me. I know now that he was a shy, tender-hearted person with a sensitive soul.

Unlike Kishirō, who was a man of fortitude, he was a weak, ordinary person. Because of this weakness I felt deeply sorry for poor Kinroku, yet sometimes I hated him so terribly that I felt like killing him with my own hands.

That summer Kinroku became weaker in the heat. He no longer knocked his body against the strong grille of the cage, and no longer shouted and bawled in a voice loud enough to shake the house. He slept constantly, his mouth slack, his body limp. Then on the morning of 2 September, he was lying dead in his dimly lit room, like an animal.

On a perfect autumnal morning, clear and pale, as I knelt on the cool tatami matting, he was lying shabbily like an old man of seventy, exposing his lean, thin, hairy legs, although he was still only thirty-three.

– 2 –

THE MEANING OF HATRED

After Kinroku's bawl ceased and the cage was taken away, an autumnal silence descended on the isolated house in the mountains, a deafening silence full of pain and agony.

Beyond the eaves, the beauty of the autumn colours on the surrounding mountains stirred my soul. I was twenty-three.

Day after day my wish to know my father became stronger. I felt an urge to learn the circumstances of my birth and the reason for my presence here.

I missed not the slightest word when my mother and nurse mentioned my father.

My father was called Sahachirō in his childhood and his early days were full of bitterness. When he was born in the castle town of Himeji, his father Yamanouchi Kageyu was a masterless samurai. The family then went up to Kyōto, but Kageyu died there when Sahachirō was only four. Then mother and son spent a wandering life in Kyōyo and Ōsaka and knew the bitterness of not even being able to get their daily bread.

Yet my grandfather Kageyu had once been a samurai in the province of Tosa with an income of 20,000 Koku. He was also a great-nephew of Yamanouchi Kazutoyo, first governor of Tosa, who had earned 240,000 Koku. Although Kageyu was destined for a sad death, he chose his own path.

Kageyu, like my father, had that unfortunate personality which was a characteristic of the Nonaka family.

I wished to know my grandfather better, because I thought his personality might have some bearing on my father's sudden disgrace and our present punishment.

Kageyu was born in 1573. He lost his father when he was seven, and grew up much loved by his mother and her uncle Yamanouchi Kazutoyo. He was allowed to assume his mother's family name of Yamanouchi and served as a retainer near Kyōto. When Lord Kazutoyo was appointed governor of Kakegawa near Edo, Kageyu was given 3,000 Koku and promoted to one of the highest posts as a chief retainer. Subsequently, when Lord Kazutoyo became governor of Tosa, Kageyu was paid 29,000 Koku in the town of Nakamura there, with the promise of an additional 1,000 Koku.

It was generally believed that Kageyu would inherit his uncle's title, although it created some ill-feeling with Shurinosuke, a younger brother of Lord Kazutoyo. Being childless, the lord regarded Kageyu as a son and expected him to marry his beloved daughter.

The death of this daughter in an earthquake did not affect Kageyu's position as heir. However when Kageyu was twenty, there had been born to Shurinosuke a long-awaited son, Tadayoshi; so that when Lord Kazutoyo became governor of Tosa, it had already been decided that the young Lord Tadayoshi was to be heir to the Yamanouchi clan.

Some years later, Lord Kazutoyo retired and died soon after, and the fourteen-year-old Lord Tadayoshi succeeded him as second governor of Tosa, with his father Shurinosuke as regent, holding the real power.

Kageyu's position thus became less important in the Yamanouchi clan, in terms of both family and power, because of these changes, and his fortune began to decline, little by little.

He had inherited from his father a large share of the severe, stern Nonaka disposition, and from his mother, an arrogance and a rash temper. He was extremely taciturn and it was normal for him not to speak to his wife and children all day if he chose. But he loved knowledge and studied the doctrine of Zen in great depth. He was also a man of refined taste who could recite a Noh play. However the Nonaka disposition was too strong to be modified by learning and meditation in Zen Buddhism.

Kageyu's wife was a sister of Ikeda Toshitaka, the lord of Himeji castle and his position in the Yamanouchi clan was bolstered by the power of the Ikeda clan behind him.

It had been decided, through Ikeda Toshitaka's mediation with Lord Kazutoyo, that Kageyu would get 30,000 Koku in Nakamura. But before this promise could be kept, Lord Kazutoyo had died, and Shurinosuke, father of the second governor, Tadayoshi, not only broke the promise but reduced Kageyu's fief to 11,000 Koku.

Too enraged to make plans about his house and property, or to consider his wife, Kageyu departed alone in a ship, as if to cast aside the province of Tosa.

He landed in Himeji and went for shelter to the Ikeda clan, but refused outright when Lord Toshitaka asked him to serve, although Toshitaka greatly desired to use his ability. Kageyu then went up to Kyōto. He had grown to hate samurai and had lost all faith in mankind. He decided he would never serve again.

His wife followed him up and died in Amagasaki. After that he remarried in Ōsaka, to Akita Manjo. From this union my father was born in the castle town of Himeji in 1615, during the time of the second Shōgun of the Tokugawa Government.

When my father was four, the iron-willed Kageyu died,

leaving his wife and son behind in one of the dirty towns of Kyōto. From then began their wandering life of hardship. Although my mother, nurse and brothers did not know all the details, the story of this period of my father's life was almost legendary.

Until Sahachirō was eleven, they led an unsettled existence in Ōsaka and its neighbourhood. Then in 1627, when he was twelve, he met in the streets of Sakai in Osaka Ogura Shōsuke, a member of the Tosa clan government.

Sakai was then a busy and prosperous commercial city, with a large trade. It also saw Dutch ships and was full of bustling activity and strange fascinating things. In the slums of the city, he and his mother lived doing piecework.

Our father told us nothing of their hard life. He had a very similar nature to that of his father and had that special Nonaka disposition – taciturn, stern, quick-tempered and iron-willed. He was always looking ahead to the future and never attempted to reflect on the past until the day he was deposed.

When he met Ogura Shōsuke, he was an impressive boy with great potential talent. His destiny was largely due to the recommendation of Ogura, who perceived the boy's ability. He was recommended to Nonaka Genba, a younger brother of his father Kageyu, who received him as a son and subsequently made him head of the Nonaka family.

It was natural for my father to enter the Nonaka household as Genba was his uncle and as his grandmother was still alive and well.

Genba was a foster grandfather to me. He was said to be one of the six most powerful Tosa officials, earning 5,980 Koku and feared by the public as a stern administrator. He arranged my father's marriage to his second daughter, Ichijo.

I have read and heard much from my mother and brothers about my grandmother Manjo. My father was devoted to her. I am sure that the greatest love of his life was not his lawful wife, Ichijo, nor our mothers and their children, but politics and Manjo. They were almost like lovers, like a couple who adored each other more than anything in the world.

Manjo probably loved my father more as a man than her own husband, Kageyu. As I read about her belief in him and her admiration of his ability, about her sharp, scathing criticism of his character and about her anxiety for his future, all of which seemed as if she had foreknowledge of his destiny, they weighed upon me and clearly implied illicit love.

The busy commercial city of Sakai was not a bad place and even a woman could manage to get money to live by her piecework. Sahachirō and his mother had settled there because she had thought the breath of prosperity in that new age would be useful for her son's future.

The long period of war came to an end at last and the third Tokugawa Shōgun became ruler. It was no longer the time when a man boasted of his tactics and achievements in battle.

When Sahachirō was asked to be the heir of Nonaka Genba, Manjo exercised all her prudence. She needed to be thoughtful and cautious about this good fortune, as they had borne hardship for so long.

Manjo believed in the superiority of her son's character. She regretted only that she could not develop it. It was an era when learning was needed. 'Whatever happens I shall not bury him in obscurity. For that I can bear even double our present hardship. However much adversity there may be in life, I shall put up with it for my son. I must.'

So my father and his mother moved to Tosa and went

to live in the imposing Nonaka Mansion, situated inside the Ōtemon, the main gate of Kōchi castle. He changed his name to Nonaka Den-emon Ryōkei.

In 1636, Genba grew ill and died and my father inherited the family title and the office of administrator. Ogura Shōsuke, who had found him, in fact proposed to the authorities of the Tosa clan that the young Nonaka Den-emon should succeed his uncle as administrator.

Shōsuke was a moderate, thoughtful and responsible official, and although of small stature he was powerful enough to suppress the chief retainers' objections to the young man.

It was Shōsuke who had lifted the finances of the Tosa clan from near-bankruptcy and revived them by his scrupulous, careful character, his mathematical brain and his patience.

He loved Den-emon, who was eagle-eyed, stern and upright, full of aspirations and ideals. He could not but love the young man whose character was almost the opposite of his own. Even after he turned his job over to his son and retired, he loved my father and watched him till he died. While the old Ogura lived, while the old man watched him, my father's political ambitions were realized one by one. His political skill was so dazzling that no hatred or jealousy could touch him.

It is so ironic and absurd for us to study that same learning which our father loved passionately and to spend our confined lives in pursuit of knowledge, because that very knowledge, Nangaku[8], inspired my father's zeal for politics, which caused this longstanding hatred against us.

My father turned from the doctrine of Zen to Confucianism. I hear it was in 1637 that Ogura Shōsuke gave him *The Doctrine of the Golden Mean* upon his return from his altenate-residence[9] period. The freshness and power of the new learning fascinated him.

Confucianism had also reached Tosa, introduced by a scholar from Suō, who had escaped wars to lead an itinerant life in the province. It was kept alive like a banked charcoal, despite apparently dying out during the long wartime period, and was handed down to the monk Jichū as Nangaku. Later Jichū returned to the world and established himself south of Kōchi, where he worked as a physician and gave classes on his teachings.

A singular feature of this learning was its new interpretation of the relationship between theory and practice. He proposed that one could put Confucianism to practical use, in order to make the country prosperous: by not despising material things; by husbanding resources and making use of learning.

My father was still young when he became an administrator for the Tosa clan, then laid waste by wars and in financial difficulty. His knowledge of this teaching cast such light on his problems that it became the basis for all his work and politics.

He searched for books on Confucianism, not only in Edo, but also in Nagasaki and Sakai. He obtained books imported from China which had no guidance for translation into Japanese and he sat late into the night trying to interpret them with his friends. At his own expense he had the few original books cut on a block and then gave them to the bookshops of Kyōto and Edo to publish.

He wanted to share with everyone his enjoyment in acquiring knowledge. Even a humble farmer or a low-born merchant could, if he wished, join in the class in the corner. The mansion inside the Ōtemon was opened to many young people every night.

I could understand my father at that time – he seemed at his finest then. He was said to inspire fear in people, for when he found fault, his gaze was hawk-like. Yet even though his eyes were scathing and stern, they must have been young, limpid and eager for knowledge at that time.

'About politics. . . .' When I began to understand what was going on around me, that phrase was always uttered by someone in the house in a gloomy way.

When mentioned by my mother and nurse it always contained a hint of secrecy, and conveyed fear, grief and resentment, so that the very phrase evoked anxiety. Mere child that I was, I knew the word played a major part in our present lot. It overshadowed me. Yet I knew only a shadow of politics, not politics itself; that is to say I only knew an obscure side of it.

I never saw what my father actually accomplished or those things he almost achieved. I know them only in the abstract because my elder brother often told me of them.

When my elder brother was alive he would relate these accomplishments as if he believed, or wanted to believe, that a knowledge of our father's work would erase the emptiness of our lifetime of imprisonment. We were taken in so easily, too, by his conviction. All my father's deeds were so great and wonderful that we were easily deluded.

The war-torn mountains and fields of Tosa and the devastated, weary minds of the upright, simple people were spread before my father, a young administrator, like the raw block put in front of an engraver to carve as he wished. And my father was fascinated by Confucianism, despite its philosophical complexities, as the technique to deal with these problems.

He worked like a man possessed. I have the list of his public works, explained to me by my elder brother.

From 1638, when he was twenty-four, until 1663 when, at forty-nine, he lost his position, labour continued unceasingly on numerous waterways and on drainage works totalling 73 miles in length, on embankments, harbours, sluices and locks.

Rivers were redirected so that the war-torn mountains and fields could be cultivated. My father was deeply impressed by the beauty and fertility of the land he developed. For him it was both the realization of an ideal and an art into which he poured all his energy.

My father also formulated a tax law. When I saw the originality, flexibility and detail of his scheme, I understood how he had developed it with more enthusiasm and sensitivity for its beauty than even a skilled craftsman for his art.

However, none of my brothers or sisters saw the actual works created by my father, so none of us understood them. (Nor do we understand why we are victims of this hatred.)

The first unlucky sign in such a forceful destiny had occurred much earlier, long before the clan lord, who trusted him absolutely, had retired.

When his beloved mother died, he conducted a pure Confucianist funeral for her, causing allegations that he was a Christian and thereby arousing suspicions of treason.

The graveyard in question was completed in two months, with the labour of one thousand men, in the quietness of a lovely wooded hillside on his estate Motoyama. He followed the coffin along the mountain path, over 24 miles, barefooted and in simple garments. It was indeed a solemn occasion. For his dear mother whom he loved almost as a wife, he must have wished to build a royal tomb fit for an emperor. He must have wanted his mother to sleep amidst the beauty he longed for.

The grandeur of the tomb and the strangeness of the Confucianist funeral created quite a stir. Before long a false rumour circulated, which spread as far as Edo, that the High Steward Nonaka had embraced Christianity, had illegally built a castle on his own estate Motoyama and thereby showed signs of treason.

When questioned by the Government, the lord of the clan, who was then in Edo for his alternate-year residence, was spurred to action. He sent an express messenger, ordering my father to go to Edo to see him. Christianity had been banned since the Christians in Shimabara had raised a riot ten years before in 1637. Secret believers were still hunted resolutely and if found, could not escape beheading or crucifixion. Any rumour about Christianity was always an omen of ill-fortune. It was a white arrow which heralded ruin.

My father hastened to Edo, day and night, still clad in mourning, to try to contradict the rumour by explaining the essence of the funeral, according to pure Confucianism. The Edo Government ordered Hayashi Razan, the official Confucian scholar, to examine my father's explanation. Razan reported that the funeral for the mother of Tosa's chief retainer accorded with orthodox Confucianist theory and had no parallel with Christianity.

Thus my father just managed to quell the doubts and was even able to see the Shōgun and return successfully. Successfully – I wonder if it was.

'It was after that I had to stay in Edo as a hostage,' said my eldest brother.

He was only three then. In that year the third Shōgun died. From about April, when the fourth Shōgun came to power, there had been indications of tension and restlessness among the people, and in July 1647, a plot by the masterless samurai was detected. My father's affair was just after that. In addition, my father was unfortunately famous enough to be thought a cunning statesman.

It was said that the lands of Tosa had a true yield of over 300,000 Koku, rather than the stated 240,000 Koku[10] and that the increase was due to my father's ability. Moreover it was ominous that my father, as a chief retainer, had been implicated by sinister words like 'Christian' and 'treason'.

At the same time, the Edo government knew that he patronized prominent weapon-makers from Sakai and other areas, and that he had established a rule for country samurai, whereby a thousand desperate surviving retainers of a vanquished lord were given work, to relieve public anxiety about their disruptiveness. It was common talk that these samurai could be mobilized by my father as a personal army if necessary. All these rumours were reported to the Government by the lord of a neighbouring clan who had been ordered to spy on Tosa.

Nevertheless, to all appearances several years passed quietly. In its ten year dispute with its adjoining clan over territories, Tosa won the lawsuit with consummate skill. The public works to utilize water from the rivers Yoshino, Niyodo, Monobe, and Shimanto were almost completed. The towns of Yamada and Gomen, set up in the newly developed areas, grew and prospered. My father was proudest of his achievements when in 1661, rebuilding commenced for the Murotsu and Tsuro harbours.

The lord of the Tosa clan and the retired lord visited my father's house inside the Ōtemon on New Year's Day, congratulated him on the success of his long-term policies and praised his distinguished services. He was granted another 1,000 Koku. In addition he was granted direct control over fifty of the country samurai. In this year I was born, his third daughter, in the house inside the Ōtemon.

Only two years later, in July 1663, my father lost his position and retired. Before the end of the year he died suddenly. I heard that he spat up blood on his deathbed, although there was a rumour that he also took poison.

Nevertheless he had long suffered from a chronic chest disease.

None of my brothers or sisters knew how he lost his position. My eldest brother, who grew up in Edo as a hostage, was called back when he was fifteen to be head of our household after my father was forced to retire. In addition, the next year, on 3 March, we were ordered into exile.

My brother knew only the little that our stubborn father would tell him and the facts which he could glean from our father's men. They knew the obvious reasons why my father was ruined. But I think the true reason might have been a surprisingly small amount of envy, or just a little rivalry.

In any event, on 19 July 1663, a statement was presented by three people – a principal retainer, Fukao Dewa, a young brother of the retired clan lord, and his son. It alleged three complaints: there was discontent with finances; there were heavy taxes on everyone, including merchants; there was harsh compulsory labour for farmers; these dissatisfactions were even causing some farmers and fishermen to desert to other clans. It further alleged that my father's policy was detrimental to the clan.

The statement was sent to my father with an accompanying letter from the lord of the clan, ordering him to engage in discussions with his three accusers, in order to moderate his policy. In it my father also noticed the signature of the retired clan lord.

For twenty-eight years he had believed the phrase 'master and servant are one flesh' referred to him and his lord. He had accomplished the difficult task of transforming the fortunes of a clan, believing that his lord had relied on him totally. Now his lord listened to accusations by incompetents, criticized his life's work and ordered him to reform his policy. He burned with humiliation, for he had not been criticized to his face for twenty-eight years and had been accustomed to act on his own authority.

He felt that all was finished. All – the beauty and harmony of Confucianist philosophy, and his passionate desire to create at least one ideal society on this earth.

On 28 July, his resignation of post was granted. On 14 September, the letter of renunciation of his position as family head was also accepted. My eldest brother was recalled from Edo and succeeded to the Nonakas. It was in the autumn, when I was three.

My father now lived apart from his family and settled in a cottage in Nakano. It was along the Funairi Canal, one of the waterways fed by the Yamada lock of the River Monobe, the lock he had completed with such difficulty and enthusiasm.

In a simple cottage by the clear, calm water, which flowed through the vast, rich, newly developed land, he avoided everyone and lived alone with an eighteen-year-old boy, Komaki Jirohachi, as his servant. Only a few books and a large vermilion-lacquered conch shell were kept beside him.

The conch shell was a visible reminder, for it had been blown as a signal for the start and end of labour on the sites where he had worked so enthusiastically. He liked it most of all. Of the books, he most enjoyed the *Songs of Ch'u*.

Now I shall read one of the cantos of *Encountering Sorrow*.

> Although I know it will surely ruin me
> If I frankly tell how mistaken is my lord,
> I cannot but tell him.
> I shall point on high and swear by God

And say how I was wholly sincere,
Not for myself, but for him.
When I first served my lord, he believed in me
  and depended on me utterly.
And my vow to be faithful to my lord
Had the strength of a nuptial tie.
Yet in the midst of my work
My lord forsook me, believing the slanders.
Alas! How terrible it is!

'Alas, why did my lord abandon me halfway through my work and believe the slanders?' – My father might well have understood the heartbreaking loyal sorrow which Ch'u Yüan felt towards his lord, the King of Ch'u.

A few days after my father resigned, on 1 August, a new rule for samurai was declared; on the 16th, a law was passed for the abolition or reduction of tax on twenty-three items for merchants; on the same day, a law for abolition or reduction of tax on thirty-nine items for farmers was passed; on 21 September, a law was passed for the repeal of forty-three items for fishermen, their ships and vessels. The structure and order of the ideal society which my father had tried to build up was destroyed completely and obliterated in a few days.

Komaki Jirohachi remained quietly with my father, who was always silent. He mentioned nothing about the fast-changing times or the administration. He was well aware of my father's state of mind.

It was one of my father's pleasures, while sitting calmly on his verandah, to see the evening breeze rippling over the Funairi Canal and the farmers pushing off in their boats full of piled up ears of rice. As the wind blew across the fields it carried the balmy scent of ripened grain.

Autumn ended and winter came. As it grew colder, my father's chest disease worsened. Jirohachi, looking after my father, grieved to see him cough sleeplessly at night. In the early morning of 15 December, he was attacked by a harsh, sudden spasm of coughing, spat up blood and died soon afterwards. He was forty-nine.

His relatives and his men guarded the coffin to bring his body back into the mansion inside the Ōtemon of Kōchi Castle. They left his cottage in Nakano and arrived at the Ōtemon in the evening. But there they were denied entry, being told by the watchman that the gate must not be defiled by a coffin. Although they patiently tried to negotiate, they could not manage to enter with it. Through the trees they could see the light of the house where he had once lived.

They had no choice but to return the same way, protecting the dead body over seven miles, even though it would take all night. In the shivering cold of December, mutely following the coffin, they came back along the road which had already started freezing. Komaki Jirohachi, who had been my father's constant companion, was observed still at his dead master's side in the solemn funeral procession, which was full of regret and bitterness.

In this way, the funeral for my father was at last held on 17 December at Komaki's house instead, near the cottage in Nakano. Under a grey sky, with snow fluttering down, the funeral proceeded towards the cemetery of Mount Takami in Kōchi. A plain wooden grave marker was erected, on which was written an ancient Buddhist inscription 'Keishoin Shukaku Nisso', 'Here lies a noble learned scholar'. The funeral finished among the trees where it was as dark as night, amidst thickly falling snow.

Jirohachi went down to a grassy place below the cemetery under cover of darkness and snow. Before leaving the house, he indirectly bade his last farewell to his mother. He had secretly beckoned her as she was busy instructing the kitchen maids and asked for one of her padded garments for him as underwear, and a cup of sake. Since his master's death he had hardly slept a wink. In the dusky back room, amidst the household bustle before carrying the coffin out, he poured sake for them both, staring at her with his reddened eyes.

The will he had written to his best friend was in his bosom.

'As I was so deeply favoured by my dead master, I wished that I might always be his servant and I wished that I might never be left behind, even for a single day should he die. I was eager to end my life immediately after him, on the night he died, without preparing for the funeral or setting matters right. But I thought people would deride me, saying that I was so confused that I hastened to die. Now that the funeral is finished, I shall kill myself tonight.

'But junshi[11] is a primitive custom of this country, and my master used to despise it, considering it unseemly for a man of honour. Yet I was the only one who remained beside him and served him day and night and my master was so good to me that I cannot repay his kindness except by following him to the grave. There is no point in continuing my life. Although I know it is against my master's will, I do wish only to follow him, even though it may be said to be the suicide of a foolish man.

'I regret that the hatred of our clan lord is deep-seated and therefore I wanted to make it clear why I killed myself as I well know it is prohibited in this country. There is no other reason. I wanted to explain that the reason I killed myself was to repay the favour of my dead master.'

When the strict order was issued to destroy the Nonaka family, deprive it of its fief and condemn its children to exile in Sukumo, it was the next year on 3 March, an auspicious day, the Girls' Festival, one of the five annual festivals.

On that day, the sturdy samurai were stationed near the mansion inside the Ōtemon; in addition, samurai were mobilized to keep watch, even on the road leading to the estate which had belonged to my father.

The action of the clan against the Nonakas was identical to that of the Edo Government in confiscating the estates of rebel daimyos and ruining their families, and it effectively created public doubt about whether or not my father had harboured rebellious designs.

My eldest brother Seishichi, aged sixteen, my third brother Kishirō who was eight; myself aged four, my youngest brother Teishirō, five months, and our mother Ike Kisa; my second brother Kinroku, fifteen, and his mother Kumon Kachi; my elder sister Yone, aged eighteen, and her mother Yana; my elder sister Kanjo, who was seven, and my younger sister Shōjo, aged three, and their mother Minobe Tsuma – all went into the house – eight children and our four mothers.

Teishirō was carried in his mother's arms and I was taken by the hand by my wet-nurse and we went into the palanquins provided. On the beach of Urado we found two boats sent around for us from the Andō family in Sukumo, where we were supposed to be exiled. The Andō held office as one of the five principal retainer families of Tosa.

On the fateful day, I, still being very young then, was probably too excited to stay still in a palanquin or boat, finding it the happiest of days, and I would have been running about among the depressed, sad adults. Although the adults were bowed down by such unrelieved fortune, it must have been something of a gay and merry change for me.

– 3 –

AN UNSEEN VISITOR

Our house was at the foot of Mt. Honjo, to the west of the Andō mansion, the former home of my foster-grandmother.

The secluded grass-thatched dwelling was surrounded by a high wall and a bamboo palisade, outside which stood a hut where the guard kept watch. The bamboo palisade was built so high that it almost reached the edge of the eaves and if it became rotten with the lapse of time, it was rebuilt.

There was a village out of sight and earshot. People were so frightened they dared not pass through this valley where lived the sinners who had shaken the world.

On one evening every year, about the end of autumn or the beginning of winter, on the mountain opposite, smoke would rise in the wind and I would observe the flames of a grass fire, like the tongue of a slithering snake. The smoke and flame would dart about from place to place all night on the slope and next morning I would find the mountain burnt deep black.

Soon afterwards I would notice the tiny figure of a man over there. The faraway figures of the villagers were, apart from the guard, the first men I ever saw from the outside world.

Strangely enough, to me as a young child, the figures

were truly dreadful. They crept about with bent bodies, wielding their hoes and sowing their seeds, on the slope of the black, burnt mountain. Yet curiosity overcame fear and I would watch their diligent, tiny, ant-like figures.

I know not why, but I could never believe they were happy. On the steep slope of the mountain, they were bent double as they wielded their hoes and crawled about in silence all day long with their baskets. They seemed forlorn and unhappy, like helpless folk whom I knew from children's tales, captured and enslaved by a mountain witch.

It was my irrational fear as a very small child that they might come down here. Even when I was wailing unreasonably for something, if I was threatened by my nurse: 'O-En-sama, if you continue such nonsense, they will come down from the mountain over there. They will come and say "Is there any crying child? I want a child crying",' I would stop in a flash, however hard I might have been wailing.

In those days I was happy and free enough. I looked up out of the bamboo palisade, onto a forbidden world into which I could not step and I was afraid of the people who lived out there and seemed so wretched.

In the spring, on the burnt mountain, buckwheat developed blue buds and then the slopes undulated in a carpet of white flowers from summer to autumn. On a beautiful moonlit night, the buckwheat-covered mountain was white and dreamy like the world of a fairy-tale told by my nurse.

Several years passed and as I grew into a woman I came to enjoy watching the labourers working on the mountain. I knew that they, who had once seemed to me unhappy and enslaved, were free people and I knew myself to be captive. I felt that an idle life bore only a superficial resemblance to happiness and I felt that the hard working peasants were less unhappy in their freedom. Once I had been frightened of the villagers, thinking that they might come and fetch me. Now as I watched them working all day, I wished they would do so.

In the small garden surrounded by the bamboo palisade, there was a pasania tree, around which coiled a wild wistaria with purple blossom in season. It never failed to bloom.

After my elder sister's death, a second bereavement occurred in 1669 when I was nine. My grandmother died, but I have no memory or impression of her, for she was cared for in the Andō mansion, with her daughter Ichijo.

However my heart went out to my father's lawful wife, Ichijo, who stayed alone with the Andō. That lady, whom I had never seen, sometimes indicated her kindness and sympathy by giving the guard some seasonal delicacies for us. When I became older, my heart reached out to her, not in gratitude for her kindness but with fellow-feeling. I wanted, harshly, to have some idea of how she had survived, because her burdensome destiny impressed me deeply.

Ichijo married my father at seventeen. He was then twenty-three; the next year he took up his post. Then, captivated by knowledge, he came across the Confucianist teaching which stated: 'Marriage within the family is harmful and should be avoided.' My father and Ichijo were related, having the same grandmother. I do not know how much he agonized. All I know is the result, that my father decided to be more faithful to his learning than to Ichijo.

He decided to live apart from his new wife and persuaded her to agree. From then on, they lived separately in the same house, like brother and sister. She lived in vain, without even having a baby, looking on while my mother and other women won his favour and bore children.

She was excluded when we were exiled, not only because she was a daughter of Nonaka Genba, but also, I imagine, because she was considered pitiable and hardly a relation of my father. When I was told the story by my elder brother, it was so touching that I said instantly, 'Alas, what a pitiful lady she is! And how cruel of him to do that!'

'Oh, no! To our father, learning was everything and it was the guiding principle by which he lived. A truth has to wait until a man bravely appears to practise it and only then can it flourish for the first time. There is no other way but to wait for a truly brave man to bring to life theory and philosophy, so that they can be clearly visible in his conduct. One must be ruthless sometimes. I rather envy the man who can find the knowledge on which he can lavish such passion.'

My brother would not meet my eye.

Like my elder brother, I envy my father because he discovered new knowledge and he was passionate enough to find in it an ideal which glowed throughout his life. His encounter with learning was so fresh and active compared with ours!

But my first doubt about my father concerned his marriage with Ichijo. I may not be able to understand the monster of politics but even I, condemned to maiden-hood, can dimly imagine a proper marriage.

Nevertheless I did not further oppose my elder brother about it at that time, because I was shocked to realize the emptiness of his life and of his devotion to knowledge, which he had kept secret from his brothers and sisters. It perplexed and confused me.

What end could learning serve us, imprisoned for life within these walls? Although I rather ill-naturedly continued to think this, the shock chilled me when I read clearly in his face the emptiness of his mind. In fact while I believed knowledge to be useless, at heart I wanted positive proof from him that it was worthwhile.

From year to year the time passed and we were still detained. Then one day in the summer of 1686 – I will never forget that day all my life – a miracle happened to us.

My eldest brother and second brother had already died, and I was twenty-six years old. What can I call it but a miracle?

None of us recognized it. It was a hot day with a blazing sun and the heavy aroma of grass hung over our house. Along the humid grassy path, a miracle quietly visited us.

Although neither villagers nor grassfires could come near us, a man appeared, a man who had walked all the way from the castle town of Kōchi to see us – over 73 miles. It was only the next day that they let us know. The guard did not tell us, but only informed an officer.

An old guard who was familiar with my elder brother said, 'Yesterday a man named Tani Tanzaburō[12] came to visit you from Kōchi. Although he wanted to be allowed to see you, he had not been granted permission by the clan Government. I told him that I could only give you his message.'

'Tani Tanzaburō? I wonder who he is? Would you know him?'

'I'm not sure, but he said he was a pupil of Yamazaki Ansai[13] He was a thin young man.'

'Oh, many thanks. If he is still there, please tell him we are indeed grateful.'

After the guard had gone, Kishirō, immediately came to me and my younger brother. We had strained our ears to hear everything and we looked at him with sparkling eyes.

His eyes were shining, too. We stared at each other in silence for a while.

It was then that I heard the name of Tani Shinzan for the first time. Nobody knew anything about him, except that he was a thin young man and a pupil of Yamazaki Ansai. But that was enough. The important thing was that a miracle had happened to us. All my family had beaming faces as they talked of the stranger.

I am sure that he had heard about my father and us from Yamazaki Ansai. So it was not only my father's political opponents who remembered us, despite our twenty-three years under house arrest. He had ventured to meet us, although he was a stranger to our world and possibly the only one who might remember us.

That fact narrowly managed to stop the disillusionment which had started to fester between my brothers and sisters, for they had lost the desire to believe in learning, which had given their lives meaning. In fact in those days I was greatly regretting that we had nibbled indiscreetly at a little knowledge. I even imagined secretly the happiness of knowing nothing and of being lovers in this cage, so that we could enjoy our lives as they were and die innocently like animals. Perhaps in our hearts, my brother and I had already violated each other like naïve and tender criminals.

A deep-rooted discontent had been engendered by the impossibility of such actions, but with the advent of the miracle man, the danger had been blown away like a nightmare. Although I was not immediately aware of it, I felt refreshed and my body became suddenly lighter. I understood this after I awoke from a dream I had in the early morning of the next day.

We had a quiet but lively conversation until late at night. At long last, after midnight, we went to bed.

A grass fire was burning all over the mountain

opposite. The fire was burning stealthily, stretching like a creature towards me. I was watching it: the tongue of a fast-moving, single line of flame was stretching towards me and I knew it was a man. I knew it was a man who I was eagerly awaiting. The flame was supposed to reach closer and closer until it came right up to my feet. Then it would turn into a puff of smoke, after which a man was supposed to appear as if by magic.

Then I became aware of standing just beside the bamboo palisade and peeping out. The tongue of flame was crawling about at the foot of it. Now I had to call out his name. If I did so, the tongue of flame would crawl over the palisade and reach me. But I could not remember his name, or rather I knew it but I could not give voice to it.

'I have to call him, otherwise he will leave. Or a guard will come and drive him away.'

Desperately perspiring, I tried to force his name from my throat, but strangely enough, my voice failed me.

I ran along the palisade, to right and left. The flame crawled quickly after me. Dear! Dear! At that moment I was so full of tension that I screamed something and a pillar of fire flared up inside my body.

I awoke bathed in perspiration. All was a dream, but inside my body the spurt of flame and the tension remained like a hot, ebbing tide. In the dream it had been that moment when a woman burns for the first time. In the darkness I writhed and gasped with the unexpectedly strange burning power inside my body.

The night wore on and I could hear the faint breathing of my mother sleeping beside me. I found I was smiling quietly. My feeling now might be described as a premonition of good fortune, or some sort of premonition of luck, or even contentment. I felt an abundance of sweet blood tingling throughout my body like softly fluttering feathers.

Although I tried, I could not erase the quiet smile. A power had spurted out from inside me and overflowed. Life flooded through me, right to my fingertips. I knew myself for the first time and I was satisfying myself for the first time.

In the sky over our house, a cuckoo flew by with a noisy shriek. I thought it would also fly, shrieking noisily, over the inn in the nearby town of Sukumo, where the man would be sleeping tonight.

I slept no more until morning. I arose earlier than everyone else and drew water from the well. At the foot of the palisade a tiny spiderwort had grown a fresh bright-blue flower, wet with morning dew. I picked it and left it in a vase on my elder brother's desk.

All day long I was silent and I might have seemed in low spirits, but my heart was inexpressively, willingly softened and I was full of happiness. I might spend all my life in this house but it would be worthwhile now that I had received the gift of life. Tears sometimes came to my eyes for no reason. On this day I thought most tenderly not only of my two dead brothers but also of all my family.

It was nearly a year later when Tani Shinzan sent a long letter to my elder brother.

I still remember that the days of that year passed more rapidly, I knew the day would surely come when we would receive a letter from him. I had no doubt at all that eventually he would try to contact us. In fact, compared with the twenty years I had already spent in the house and the twenty which were to follow, why would one year be long?

It was not long at all, for no letter could be sent to us without permission of the clan Government and here, over 73 miles from the castle town of Kōchi, at the disease-ridden western end of Tosa, even men seldom passed by.

With great excitement, we drew nearer and watched as my elder brother's fingers opened the envelope.

> I studied *Elementary Learning* when I was nine. It was a few years later, after the former administrator (our father) had died, that I discovered his children lived in Sukumo. I tried secretly to learn something of them. I attempted to contact people who had served his family, but to no avail, due to their changing fortunes.

From the words written there, we knew for the first time how we were perceived by the world outside this house. Out there we were still spoken of with caution and the political hatred towards us had not yet cooled.

In addition we now knew that our father's life-long passion had not been entirely destroyed, even at the hands of heartless men. We knew too that this passion was great enough to be still manifest to a man living over a generation after my father had died, and for him to respect and love my father.

> However, being greatly disturbed by certain events during the past year, I decided to travel to Sukumo. I was delighted that my longstanding wish would be fulfilled. But to my surprise the house where they lived was surrounded by a high palisade and those whom I thought servants were warriors. I could not refrain from sighing deeply in disappointment. I felt such pity for them that my tears flowed freely. I said to myself: 'For seventeen years I have known of these people and have wished to see them. Now at last having travelled so far, I find that it is impossible. Alas, that this should be the will of Heaven.' I begged one of the guards to

> give me some poems written by Nonaka's children and they were indeed worthy of their father. But my heart was broken to learn of their pitiable lives. Even now, my thoughts are too tangled, and I am too distraught to express my feelings.

When we were arrested we were innocent children. Since then over twenty years have passed.

I am sure he was astonished, knowing that the grand Andō mansion was my grandmother's home, to see that we were living in a solitary house in a ravine which appeared to be a haunt of foxes and badgers, a house far from a village, surrounded by a high bamboo palisade and guarded by warriors. He had requested that even if he were not permitted to talk with us, we might be able to look at and silently greet each other, but in vain.

As he walked back along the humid, scented, grassy path, I am sure he repeatedly sighed and turned his head towards the palisade. We were all overjoyed to learn of his request for some of my elder brother's poems and that he had been so impressed by them. We knew for the first time that our words had touched a man outside our world.

> I am twenty-five years old now. I should be full of youthful vigour. But I am often attacked by giddiness and my ears ring and I am too unhealthy to be called a young man. I am a masterless samurai: as I am not serving the clan Government, needless to say I receive not the slightest allowance. Even so, I am sometimes criticized by them for my speech and behaviour. If I should die suddenly, I would not be able to complete the learning on which I have worked so hard, and I fear I could not pass on my knowledge. For that reason I have expressed my thoughts to you. I know that all I

have written here is illogical and that I cannot express my emotion. But I was so anxious to see you that afterwards I could not prevent myself from writing. Please burn this after you have finished reading.

We read over the letter again and again. Even after we had finished, we could not throw it in the fire. How could we do such a thing?

We pored over it with an indescribable yearning and some fear. In the town where this letter was written, political hatred for us still thrived after twenty years. Each time we re-read it, we were trying in apprehension to ascertain that.

Strangely enough, I even felt a surreptitious pleasure in doing so. It cleared away the dreadful uneasiness that here at the end of Tosa, we might sink into the oblivion which was deep in our hearts, but which no one would mention.

We could bear over twenty years of house arrest. We could bear the unyielding, heartless hatred. But I do not think we could bear such an insult, that we be forgotten and slip into oblivion, because the sole reason we lived was 'to bear the hatred'. Moreover, the remarks in his letter, 'Needless to say I receive not the slightest allowance. Even so I am sometimes criticized by them for my speech and behaviour' told of the political climate, and without knowing why, his life fired me with enthusiasm.

I knew it well. From then on I started living through him, through that poor, thin young Confucianist scholar called Tani Tanzaburō. . . .

The man was already mine. I knew very well how much I wanted him. Nobody was aware of the many emotions I felt for him. Of course even my elder brother had no idea.

After that, time started flowing in this house. For

twenty years time had stood still and stagnated, but now it started moving. We exchanged letters regularly. Although there could be only one trip a year over a distance of 73 miles, over mountains and rivers, the time flew like an arrow because of it.

The exchange of letters was permitted only for questions and answers about books and our prose and poetry. Although sent to my elder brother, they always contained some replies to my questions. Even though there might be just a couple of lines, or ten lines or so at most for me, I could understand them as if they filled pages. The shorter and simpler the words and the more restricted they were to the confines of learning, the more freely and extensively I could read his mind.

He knew me already as a woman hidden by destiny. Now he must have known what the woman thought, grieved and suffered, living in this house for twenty years. He must have known what books she was reading, her longings and her sorrows. I wonder if the young man and I did not secretly collude and inexplicably try to read each other's minds in those letters.

When Kishirō died after being ill for only forty days or so, it felt like a punishment, as if I were being given a crushing blow. I believed that Heaven punished my insubordination.

My elder brother and I had been close companions and friends, complementing each other like husband and wife, quite apart from physical love. If someone should tell me that a wife's grief at the loss of her husband is deeper than mine, then I would refuse to believe it. I wished that I could be put in his coffin and buried with him. When I thought of the house arrest continuing far on to the end of my life, I was quite mad with despair.

I resisted the impulse to cry out or cling to the coffin as the warriors carried it away and I continued to sit upright. Even my mother did not cry in front of them. The survivors of the Nonakas were schooled too well by both death and ill-luck.

It was 11 April 1698. He was forty-two. We could barely peep through the bamboo palisade to see my elder brother's coffin carried away on the warriors' shoulders along the narrow path. The mountains were glistening with fresh greenery and the emerald colour was reflected in the paper sliding doors of the house and on my bare feet. I was thirty-eight. I looked fixedly at the blue veins rising on the back of my hands, on which the fresh green was reflected.

Now for the first time, I was trying alone to write a letter to Master Shinzan. It was my duty to tell him of the death of my elder brother and to thank him for the kindness he had shown him while he was alive. But so full of emotion was my writing, that it broke down my reserve. In truth I wanted to throw myself in front of him, cry out and complain.

> I was a child when I came to this house. Thirty-five years have passed since then. My eldest brother and my second brother have died already. Now I have lost my third brother, on whom I relied and whom I respected as if he were my own life. Who else can give me the strength to live on in this prison? At midnight I wet my sleeves with tears, my heart bursting with grief. While my third brother lived, he respected you more than I can say. It is tragic, I feel, that he must have died deeply regretting that he had not seen you. I resolved to tell you of this and so took up my pen. I beg you to pardon my humble writing. I trust you will accept the gratitude which my elder brother felt for you.

A long, respectful reply was sent to me from the

teacher, lamenting my brother's death and praising him for his ability and his virtuous character.

From then on, between us, a very thin line of communication was established. There were fewer than half the number of letters and they were much shorter than when my elder brother lived. Nevertheless by relying on those few letters, I was able to bear the last five years of house arrest.

During those five years two more deaths occurred. One was that of poor old Ichijo, who had been cared for by the Andō and the other was the death of my dear youngest brother Teishirō – the longest surviving of my brothers.

When I think of those forty years, the deaths pile up around me like rotting leaves – my eldest sister, my eldest brother, my second brother, my third brother, my youngest brother, my foster grandmother, my three step-mothers, Ichijo and several of our servants.

Now death is quite familiar to me. The dead know well that they existed merely in order to die. Although they have lost the form of men, they still sit up among us in this dilapidated house, just as when they were alive. We survivors feel their presence, here and there, just as before.

We remain now in this decaying, deserted house, with its rotten ground sills and its collapsing eaves and worn out paper sliding doors: my mother, aged eighty-one and my nurse Nobu, sixty-five, with me and my two sisters, all over forty.

We survivors wordlessly draw nearer each other, among the dead who silently float and move about us, and in the chill of autumn we feel the warmth of each other's breath.

Only then was the pardon granted, when all the yearning, the agony and the expectation of freedom had faded and withered away.

All my father's political opponents must be dead by now. The revenge of those people, insulted by my father when he acted on his own authority with arrogance and integrity, was now at last complete, so long after both my father and his opponents had died. Nonaka Den-emon Ryōkei's blood was extinguished and his three daughters were thrown out into faded, withered freedom, like grasshoppers at the end of the summer.

This is the culmination of their unyielding hatred. I cannot but smile, coldly and faintly.

One morning, we decided to walk towards the noise, a mysterious sound which had enchanted us since we were young, and quite unlike the noise of the wind or the breeze in the pine trees. We had always been taught that it was the sound of a stream.

Whether it sounded near or far, whether whispering or roaring, it had created a continual yearning from our childhood onward. Now we were released and walked towards it. My heart was beating slightly faster with emotion. The guard house was empty and silent and the valley, filled with dying autumn-tinted grasses, was wet with morning dew.

Cutting across the grassland and going down the hill, through the small pine trees, an alarming, booming sound came nearer and seemed to pressure and envelop us. We looked at each other with frightened eyes and stopped, hand in hand. The grassy hill led us to a cliff, beneath which the river was rushing. There it changed into a torrent and cascaded down like a foaming white cloth. And the roar around there reverberated like an animal howl.

The morning sun was directly behind us, shining beyond the grassy slope to glisten in the water on the far side. In the shade and the sun the river seemed to have two quite different qualities. In the sun it seemed alive, sparkling like crushed jewels, changing to blue, yellow and red, and creating bubbles. It was so beautiful and strange that I could not believe it was real.

We uttered a short cry and wordlessly continued to watch, entranced by that mysterious, beautiful form. Ever-changing, ever-restless, it was beyond my imagination. I hear that a river can sometimes take a man's life. Indeed it would be impossible not to accept death in such a fascinating stream. No wonder a river is wild when it has this force.

An exciting thought struck me. In my wonderment at the ever-changing form and colour of the running water, I imagined it was both the outside world itself and a symbol of freedom. So, in the outside world, everything would exist with its own shape and its own life, quite unlike that which I had imagined for forty years.

With a new urgency, I felt I must go to Kōchi at the earliest opportunity. The teacher held a special place in my heart and since the pardon he had been constantly in my thoughts. I was going to live. My emotion and the morning chill of the grassland caused me to shiver.

'O-En-sama, you look deathly pale,' shouted my sister, glancing behind at me.

'Kan-sama, you too,' I shouted back at her, above the noise of the rapids. We three sisters had pale faces, goose-flesh and the colour drained from our lips.

I thought of Kishirō and my younger brother, Teishirō of the gentle spirit. I wished that Teishirō could have glimpsed such a beautiful sight and that I could have watched it with Kishirō. But to have such thoughts was very foolish and meaningless. As long as they had lived the pardon would not have been granted.

A cold smile, like a nervous tic, sprang up from the pit

of my stomach. With my lips still quivering, I looked down at the shining stream. However I tried I could not control the quivering smile, until it almost became a sob.

At the same time I experienced a new warm sensation in my body, like the thawing of frozen blood, like solid cramped muscles and joints loosening and stretching, or like being tickled. I felt like laughing; I felt like crying; I felt like lying on the ground, screaming and biting the earth.

Could this be the freedom of the outer world for which I had yearned? Now these sensations became almost unbearable, storming my senses. The three of us, with tears running down our blanched cheeks, silently climbed the grassy hill in the sunshine.

Very soon, a few days after the pardon, an old man called Iguchi Kurobe'e visited us. After his 73-mile journey across mountains and rivers, the strong old man was covered in dust. Mother and nurse were speechless as they grasped his hands.

One of my father's former retainers, he lived at Asakura, a small village about two miles west of Kōchi. He was the man on whom my mother now wished to rely. His eldest son Chōsaemon had been secretly engaged in trying to obtain a pardon for us, the surviving family, after we had been sent into exile. But he had been discovered and sent into exile himself to Motoyama, where my grandmother was buried, and had lived there as a peasant. The old man went on to relate that his son had also now been pardoned and had returned to Asakura.

He talked all night as if to pour forth the anger of decades. From his story I realized that not only Chōsaemon but many other people had become victims through my father: the Confucianists whom he had educated and the samurai he had cared for were all affected.

Furthermore there was a story which fixed itself in my mind. It was beyond belief and something which even my brothers might never have conceived. Truly, it was astonishing.

'Our master was very unlucky. He exercized his ability with too much intelligence and power. He was too clever merely to fit into the Tosa clan,' the old man told us.

'If our clan lord had been sufficiently strong-willed, our master could have helped him to deliberate on the most important affairs of state for the Edo Government and he could have employed his great knowledge of statecraft to influence the whole of Japan. Then, as our master used to say, "a fine country with a philosophy in which learning was put to practical use" would have been born. In Edo, there has been no one like our master with such ability, either then or now. It was most unfortunate for him that our clan lord had neither courage nor broad vision,' he lamented. 'As our master lived in the small province of Tosa, his ability and talent caused such jealousy that he was swept away by the slanders of petty officials.'

Of course I did not know how intelligent the administrators of the Edo Government might be or how politics was conducted. But according to my eldest brother, who grew up as a hostage in Edo until he was sixteen, the Shōgun was a man without equal when planning a far-sighted scheme. He always controlled the finances of the clans and many plucky daimyō were filleted and made powerless by him in order to give his descendants peace.

It had been said that my father's splendid political ability in increasing Tosa's actual land yield from 240,000 to 300,000 Koku had incurred the disapproval of the Edo Government and led to his disgrace. If my father had taken part in national politics, his destiny would have invited far greater tragedy. I was terrified just to think of it.

Of course, if my father had deemed it possible to dominate affairs of state on the stage of Japan, his desire for an ideal world, ruled by a philosopher-statesman, might have been half-realized on a far grander scale than that of Tosa. He might have been granted more honour and contentment than he had in that fateful year of my birth, 1660.

But I think it cannot be denied that equally great misfortune might well have attacked him. Instead of my entering that house in the arms of my nurse, my short life might have been sacrificed.

He was too idealistic to live with the complex, strange, many-headed dragon of politics. Being a man who worked ceaselessly, a man of integrity and passion, he could not manage such a dragon.

I dared not say anything of this to the old man Iguchi. Secretly I pitied my father for risking such danger in pursuit of an ideal, like a moth burning itself in a lamp.

Listening to Iguchi talk, I realized that he too had a stubborn, strong character and that he had revered my father for his accumulated achievements. My father's very existence was still vital to him. I could understand that happiness might vary for different people, as I had experienced my own particular happiness under arrest. I did not want to spoil his dream.

The visit of the old man gave us courage and the one and only person on whom we could depend. We had thought vaguely that we would go back to Kōchi, the very idea of which made us feel helplessly adrift. My older and younger sisters therefore wished to stay here. Their attachment to this place, under the protection of the Andō, was mostly due to their uneasiness at not being able to imagine life in the unfamiliar castle town. But, given this opportunity, I also understood that they, as my half-sisters, wanted to live separately from me, a residue from our forty long, stifling years in this house.

In my heart I loved my sisters although they disliked books and preferred needlework and kitchen chores. I liked the ease which I felt when I was with them. I wished that I could always feel that peace.

Nor did they dislike me. On the contrary, after all our brothers died, my sisters turned their reliance and respect toward me. Just as they had attended on our brothers, they now found it enjoyable to attend around my desk.

But the ease I felt when I was with them lasted only for a time; soon it became unbearable. I became irritated. Endlessly, every day, they found it enjoyable to be totally absorbed in the smallest details of their needlework and kitchen tasks. Their undoubting composure irritated me. I wonder if it could have been because I so envied them their unquestioning acceptance of detention and their peaceful womanly lives.

Just as they treated me with respect, so I too could not help being concerned about them. It must have been imparted to them unconsciously.

'O-En-sama, you surpass men. We would like to entrust you with our family responsibilities.'

When my elder sister said this, on her knees with a low bow, and my younger sister also bowed to me, I grasped their feelings – their excessive reliance on me and at the same time, a faint distaste. That distaste had dripped silently during forty years of house arrest to collect deep in their hearts. And I pondered with irony that I was relied upon, as I surpassed men.

Moreover if my sisters stayed in this place, those who had died here would avoid feeling deserted. I would go back to Kōchi, the idea of which had, in life, haunted them all with endless affection, bitterness and longing.

I did not even know where Kōchi was, exactly, but I

wished to go where many people lived, with their hates, loves and deceptions.

Following my mother's advice I wrote a letter to the Honourable Yamanouchi Kurando, so that we might obtain some assistance from him to achieve our desire. He was one of the administrators at that time and distantly connected with us. Iguchi was expected to take the letter to him.

After the old man had gone, promising that he would make ready his house for us to visit, we started preparing for our departure. We sewed hand coverings and leggings. With cotton cloth presented by the Andō I made a wadded garment for my mother. And we carefully chose and shared with each other those worn-out, ragged clothes which we thought still useful.

In one of the following restless, busy days, I received my first letter since the pardon, from the gentleman who even then never left my thoughts. I asked the express messenger to wait and quickly penned a reply, amidst the disorder.

Most respectfully to Tani Tanzaburō,

I thank you kindly for your letter. It gladdens me to learn that you are in good health. Since you have written, we received our pardon and I am sure you will understand my telling you that I shed tears when I think with affection of the old days. As I am but a foolish woman and I have no one to consult, it is inexpressibly difficult to make decisions myself. I shall first journey to Asakura, with mother, who is over eighty, and my nurse. We shall depart as soon as possible. On my arrival I would dearly like to call upon you to seek your advice.

I beg you to give me every assistance.

Respectfully yours, En

24 September

I was hoping to depart immediately as I have already asked Kurando for permission to go to Asakura, but my plans are not proceeding as quickly as I wish.

Very sincerely

From the day after I sent the letter, we had hoar frosts every morning. Each day, a bell seemed to be ringing in my heart.

On the day preceding the departure, I tidied the house. At the foot of the bamboo palisade, I burnt the old deeds and papers, which had been handed down through the family – there were some honourable mentions given to the second in line, who had been praised for his feats of arms, and many honours which had passed through three generations, from my great-grandfather to my foster-grandfather and to my father. But I had no regrets at throwing them all in the fire.

Indeed I found it satisfying to do so.

Though such things might be important to men, they were worthless to me. Even the family name of Nonaka itself no longer had any meaning for me. I did not want to be restricted by these ties.

(My dear brothers, can you see what I am doing now? As you were men, you could not live. You had to die so that you could let me survive. Now look at the way I shall live.)

I felt no reluctance at burning everything, except those things which I could change into money later and the things which would be necessary for our livelihood. Wafting on the wind, the lavender-coloured smoke blew through the torn paper sliding door, into the empty house filled with my brothers' regrets, and drifted on. It floated out of the house again toward the late autumn-tinted woodland on Mt. Honjo. Only the ashes were heaped up;

only the black fragility of waste papers remained.

All that was left at the bottom of my cloth box were several of Kishirō's verses and letters from my teacher.

It was a morning of severe hoar frost in the latter half of October when we left the house.

Dressed in our travelling attire, we went into the castle town of Sukumo and called upon the Andō to express our thanks for the assistance they had given us during our long imprisonment. The Andō offered us the protection of a young man to accompany our women's journey, so attended by him, we left the castle town behind. We seated my mother in a palanquin, while we walked.

My two sisters came as far as the outskirts of Sukumo to bid us farewell. When we parted there, I found it so painful and so lonely that I felt my heart would break. I felt exceedingly sad and troubled for those who were remaining behind. They shed many tears and watched us until we were out of sight.

I asked the young man to take us to the Kōdo Dam, constructed by my father on the River Matsuda. Long ago when Master Shinzan had made his fruitless visit, he had stood alongside this dam on his return journey and in his letter he had mentioned being deeply moved. I wished to stand on the same spot just once. That was also my first encounter with my father, as it happened, an encounter with the longstanding hatred and the first meeting of several that I would experience on occasion from now on.

The dam, said to be one of his most complex works, was completed four years before my father lost his position, and despite being buffeted by wind and snow for over forty years, the rich water gleamed quietly and peacefully still. The bamboos with which my father had thought to conserve the bank, now created a beautiful thicket along the shore. The branches drooped and appeared hazy against the sky. Throughout the forty years that we had borne that hatred, the bamboos had grown larger here every spring. Just the vegetation, nothing else.

'At the foot of the mountain over there is the Arase Canal, built by Master Kenzan' (my father had been known by several titles), the young man said, pointing. 'People called it the perilous mountain with the soaring rock wall and it was said that the stone was virtually impossible to cut.' I heard how, even on a day of heavy snow, my father had not allowed the workmen to halt their compulsory service. He related that my father had said 'I shall only let them rest if the river is frozen and covered with snow' and, standing in the snowstorm, had directed the farmers himself.

'The children here still sing "Freeze the snow, freeze the hail" when they play handball. I hear it originated from the farmers who sang the rhyme when their work was so unbearable.'

The young man, who had no idea of their suffering, unconcernedly told us this story, probably passed on from his grandparents to his parents. I nodded silently, still facing the dam.

'Thanks to him the villages, which used to be very poor and visited by floods every year, became pleasant places to live in, enjoying rich harvests. In the villages Kenzan is spoken of as a god, for in politics he had the foresight to gaze a hundred years ahead.'

I smiled drily.

Their children and grandchildren enjoy good harvests, yet their ancestors may well have shortened their lives. At this moment I believe firmly that my own life is the most important. Just as I only live once, so did they only have one life. . . .

I do not wish to be made a victim of any greatness.

This, my secret resolution, I shall probably never disclose till I die.

The mountain slopes were almost dormant. On the sunny side of the mountain those last late-tinted leaves seemed aflame in the setting sun. We frequently caught a ferryboat to cross a river. While we waited for a ferry to return from the opposite bank, my mother would come out of the palanquin to watch it, slightly raising her sedge hat. For those of us unused to walking, it was a difficult road, but as we had recourse to palanquin and boat it was our first interesting journey.

Although we were not able to see the harbours of Kashiwajima or Okinoshima, we were able to view several of the big dams and drainage schemes along the Nakasuji and Shimanto rivers. From one dam, the Asō, nearly 4 miles of channels irrigated 200 acres of rice fields. Another conduit was taken from the dam to supply the town of Nakamura and 147 acres of surrounding farmland.

Nakamura was the place where my grandfather had once lived with a fief holding of 20,000 Koku. We stayed one night in this gracious town. Full of emotion, I recalled that it was part of the estate of the Yamanouchi, whose ancestor, Shurinosuke, my grandfather had resisted until he died. And just like my grandfather, who sailed in anger from the harbour of Shimoda, we too caught a boat there. We parted from the young man of the Andō there, at Shimoda. As we had journeyed for several days together, he was very much loath to leave us, asking if it would not be possible to attend us as far as Kōchi.

The sea was calm. But when we arrived at the harbour of Suzaki, after a whole day on the water, I continued by land as my mother had been seasick on the boat. From there the route led to the River Niyodo, on which were the Kamata Dam and the Hiro-oka Canal. This canal and the many channels running from the dam supplied nearly 4,000 acres. All was completed forty years ago, and the water had run innocently and quietly and never stopped for a moment since that time. Only with man are there changes of life, death and extremes of fortune.

I was told that this water flowed into Urado Bay like the Funairi Canal which ran through the village where my father died. Deeply moved, I stood on the bank and watched it.

Although those constructions were less than half of my father's creations, I truly thought when I saw the record of his painstaking work with my own eyes, that his happiness was more important to me than his fame. As an administrator he had enough success to cause his political opponents such jealousy that they slandered him and persecuted us, his surviving family.

'His achievements were not for himself but for the people,' my elder brother used to say. But I wonder if there is any difference between the two – the ideal enforced on others and his own ambitions.

Although my elder brother had said the works were all for the farmers' benefit, when they were created so fast, by slavery which seemed to shorten their lives and in poverty which made them abscond from the clan, I wonder if there is any difference between the ideal and the ambition. In a corner of my heart I have a vivid awareness that, though imprisoned for forty years, I am no better than his political opponents, for none of us can forgive his ambition.

I can understand half their feeling against him. But I will not allow their hatred for us. That day will never come, as long as I live.

Yet if the traces of my father's policy were mercilessly and surely to remain for hundreds of years, then all their jealousy and revenge and my forty years of resentment would be trivial and but a momentary ripple on the water.

I rested at a tea-house, stayed at an inn and observed with curiosity many people, such a variety of people of such diverse occupations. Each one never failed to surprise me. Every time, in amazement, I thought, 'Oh goodness,' and soon I thought 'Ah, that's how men behave!' A picturebook likeness, no matter how good, was not alive. In the same way, those people whom I thought I had known well from books, seemed quite different before my eyes.

Happiness could never be the same colour and shape for men of such varied occupations, with such different ideas and such different needs. And if politics were supposed to give happiness and contentment to all those people. . . .

Having grown up under house arrest, my ideas about man and life were truly shaken and rejected now that I observed people who were really living.

All those whom I saw on the journey were cleverer and far more knowledgeable than I, and above all, they were actually living. Deep in themselves they had the power to live. Expectations and uncertainties about how I would live from now on were spreading within me.

– 4 –

LEARNING TO LIVE

Before going to Asakura itself, we made a detour into the town of Kōchi, as my mother wished to see the castle.

It was evening when we went into the castle town. The row of shops had not yet been lit and still reflected the glow of sunset. I tensed slightly as I watched the people busily coming and going along the street.

Greeted by the old man Iguchi, we stopped our palanquins to look up at the castle. The three-storied castle tower rose high above the thick woods, with the sweeping curves of its steep roofs silhouetted in the afterglow and its white walls coloured pale crimson by the sunset.

Such beautiful architecture, with its clear, fresh outlines, is essential in order to display power and authority. This fine, lofty building is needed to give birth to the monster of politics. The tall, graceful edifice created my father's whole political career and led to his downfall, created the slavery by which farmers sacrificed their lives and caused our dreadful imprisonment.

The castle stood there, perfect, towering up as the symbol of irresistible, absolute power. The more merciless the politics, the more beautiful it would be. And the more cruel the politics, the more gracefully the castle would enjoy its heartless brilliance above the full-bloomed haze of cherry blossoms. I am sure it would have been so at the climax of my father's fame and on the day we were exiled.

The third clan lord had long since died, as had the fourth clan lord after him. Now the fifth lord, Toyofusa, had succeeded to the guardianship of the castle, but I felt that the meaning of the citadel would never change.

My mother and nurse had yearned so long to return that now they almost bowed down and prayed. With shining eyes, they recalled the splendid mansion of the Nonakas, which was just down in the castle grounds, inside the Ōtemon.

I, however, had other thoughts: Master Shinzan lives somewhere in this castle town. Since March last year, he has been official teacher for the clan, lecturing on Confucianism and astronomy. While I am standing here, he must be somewhere in this same town.

It was dark when we came onto the river path, so the three palanquins were lighted.

Although the village of Asakura was lost in the darkness, a bright bonfire was lit in the garden of the Iguchis. And outside the gate, people with lanterns marked with the family emblem were standing in a row and waiting for us.

When I climbed out of the palanquin and stood in the garden, I caught the odour of wet straw and the steamy, sweet smell of horses' urine from somewhere close. There was a hum of whispering, voices of women at work in the kitchen, and I felt many eyes gazing at me from the shadows and darkness in the corner of the garden. There rose up in me a defensive attitude. Wretchedly I wondered whether it was habit, after forty years under arrest, or something thrust upon me by other people.

In the parlour we accepted the congratulations of Chōsa, dressed in a crested ceremonial coat, and sat at tables for a heartwarming celebratory dinner. Unlike his father, who seemed to be very determined and took an active part in the conversation. Chōsa spoke quietly in a low voice. He looked older than his age and made me feel that he was a man who had been long overshadowed by misfortune. He gazed at me only once, instead constantly lowering his eyes and speaking only to my mother. That made an impression on me.

Although the house was large, the Iguchis were clearly poor peasants.

Across the road, in the forest was Konomaru Shrine, said to be the ancient site of an imperial palace. I gathered that my father's estate, Motoyama, was at one of the foothills of the Kitayama Mountains which ranged across the horizon, folding their dark blue slopes in the indigo sky of early winter.

I became unexpectedly involved in the bustle of my surroundings. People on the fringe of old loyalties visited us every day. Almost all were old men, who left after long talks with my mother and nurse. The same topics were repeatedly discussed. It made me tired and annoyed, whereas I was waiting for only one person and he would not appear for me.

When I finally realized that our relationship was that of teacher and pupil and that I should call upon him to express my compliments, I felt as if I would take wing.

But the old man, troubled, shook his head and restrained me, 'I think you would do better to refrain from such a thing. A castle town is censorious about everything – it's said that O-En-sama is back. She is said to be very beautiful. She is said to be over forty but looks little older than thirty – so it is persistently rumoured among the women in the castle town. You would do better to be concerned about how the world speaks of you, to avoid unexpected misfortune befalling you and others. If you heed your station as a woman, you should not think lightly of going to see a man.'

I understood the reason why the townsfolk had such an interest in me. I had already perceived it in the eyes of the old retainers who had come to visit us. Their eyes held a tinge of curiosity to view some odd creature, rather than sympathy for a woman of sad destiny. I should have been ready for the fact that a maiden of forty-three, with unshaven eyebrows, unblackened teeth and still in a long-sleeved kimono,[14] would be exposed to cruel eyes just like a deformed woman in a sideshow.

I understood what he wished to say; that the teacher would be embarrassed if such a woman should visit him. And he dropped me a hint that it would not only be on everybody's lips but it would also affect his position.

When the old man found a reliable messenger for me, I sent my first letter to the teacher from here.

'Several days have passed already since I came to Asakura. Once I arrived, I believed that I could fly over to see you. But events do not happen as I desire. Now I know, to my sorrow, that it is a most difficult world. Although I am sure you have much to occupy you, I would like to meet you. I await your visit with eagerness.'

However the letter had just been sent when the teacher's wife called upon me.

When Chōsa's wife informed me of this, in surprise I asked her to repeat it. Thoughtlessly, I had never considered his wife and I had never imagined that she would come to see me.

Of course it was not that I thought he had no wife. I did not dare to think about his wife. Why was it necessary to think of his wife?

As an ill-fated woman, expecting to finish my life under house arrest, the teacher had existed for me only as a letter, reaching across 73 miles, over mountains and rivers. And he had belonged to me entirely.

Even as my nurse was smoothing my hair style, I felt agitated and I knew I was pale.

Bowing slightly, his wife came into the parlour with a boy of about five. Although she was not tall, she was sturdily built and had a round face with a healthy complexion. Because of her clear gaze, her smile showed her intelligence. Her words of lament for my dead brothers and her appreciation of my sorrow were not quite fluent, but I could feel that her sincerity was genuine.

I listened to her speak: the teacher cannot sleep peacefully because his studies are reaching a peak; unfortunately he is too busy to call just now, although he would like to pay his respects to you and your mother. I have come to apologize on his behalf, although, simple woman that I am, I cannot act for him. He will visit as soon as he is able.

I realized that there was a custom in the world which substituted a wife for her husband. I felt a repulsion for it. How could I submissively accept something so strange? I was aware that while understanding her words, my heart bled somewhere.

Further there rose in me a sense of embarrassment which gradually compelled me to lower my gaze. Now unexpectedly in the presence of his wife, rather than the man for whom I had waited so long, I was clearly aware of the teacher himself in her. It was curiously fresh. How strange is the special relationship between a man and his wife! Although she was not the teacher, she sat before me, sharing his physical identity. She was there, not with the same mind or thought, but with the fresh, raw sensation of his body, almost as if they were one flesh.

For me, her presence was a cruel substitute. And his presence in her was far from the true, gentle state of her mind. I knew in a flash how natural it was for a wife to visit someone on behalf of her husband. For someone in my position, learning just this lesson left a scar.

Then one day, quite unexpectedly, he called upon me.

He appeared, quite without warning. All the Iguchis were out working and my nurse was, unusually, out to visit an acquaintance. Only my mother and I were in the house.

On the dark earth floor, a black shape was standing silhouetted against the dazzling midday light of a balmy autumn day. I could distinguish neither his face nor his age.

As I knelt at the door sill, an astonished sound escaped from the lips of the silent figure and struck me.

'Oh, so you are Lady En!'

I was completely taken aback.

In my heart I had been foolish enough to hope for his visit. I knew not why, but now I had lost my mental preparation. The teacher's visit would be largely impossible, I thought. Such resignation absorbed me during those days.

As his low voice called my name, it pierced me, body and soul.

A woman might have her name called in a special way only once in her life by a man. . . . I felt that in his low, strong voice, 'Oh, so you are Lady En!'

I grew weak-kneed and sank lower in shock, wordlessly staring at the black faceless figure.

Instantly I knew that those few moments of our encounter were equal to the twenty years that I had known him under house arrest.

I had spent twenty years under arrest, firmly believing that he was mine. But when I knew that over twenty years equalled only this moment, I realized for the first time that a man and a woman could never have a relationship without meeting each other.

When I led him into the room and he stepped over the sill, after brushing the dust off his socks in a free and easy manner, a strong masculine odour enveloped me. I was stupefied for a moment, holding my breath.

From behind, I watched him greet my mother. He was of thin, poor build, a small man who looked even elderly. I remembered the ageing of my eldest brother and I experienced some confusion.

Yet I felt him to be unrestricted, taking things easy and not concerned with appearances. Because of this relaxed quality, the back view of this small, poorly-built man did not seem so insignificant.

His thin, sallow face was marked by thick eyebrows. From under them, his round eyes gazed at us gently.

The exhausting nature of the long journey had caused my mother to be frequently bedridden, deprived her of her appetite and made her rambling and talkative. In a familiar manner she bewailed long the misfortune of her dead sons. Gradually the tale changed and she informed him that she could not continue to depend on the Iguchi family and that she needed her own home.

Because she had become child-like and helpless due to continual illness, she was frequently urging me to arrange for a house to be built. With each morning the frosts were becoming more severe. In this temporary dwelling, where it seemed as if the sweet smell of cow and horse urine would stain fast in my body, I looked after my mother's bodily functions. It was I who thought constantly about a house of our own. But in this new world where I was feeling my way, I felt uneasy even about trying to purchase a plot of land.

Nodding his head at the old woman's complaints, he consoled her that she would have her own home before long if only she would not distress herself. And he cheerfully related to us how he had lived in poverty since he was a child.

For generations, in the time of the Chōsogabe clan, the Tanis had been a leading family and the chief priests of their most holy shrine. But after the Chōsogabes were overthrown, the Tanis also sank in the world. When he was a child his family was in the depths of poverty, sometimes without oil for lighting and at times lacking three meals a day. He was sickly from birth and in addition, through lack of nourishment during childhood, he was afflicted with a severe eye disease. He was still troubled by weak sight.

Even when he grew up, as he had mentioned in the letters sent to us under house arrest, he sometimes had 'stomach pains and spitting of blood so severe that heaven and earth grew dark'. He told us lighthearedly of all his misery and of becoming a herbalist and a medicine pedlar, which had enabled him to journey to Sukumo to see us, and of the letter he had written to his friend in Kyōto, saying that unless they took to thievery, his family could barely survive. It was all related so gaily and innocently, as if these events had happened to someone else that even my mother, in spite of herself, burst into laughter.

'I arranged even my father's funeral in a kimono and a haori jacket I borrowed from my friend. Rich or poor, we can all survive in this world. We have no need to worry.'

He looked so strangely old for his years that I could not have ascertained his real age. Gazing at him, I wondered if it could be because he had been cursed by poverty and poor health, but I thought at the same time he gave the impression of a man who had not surrendered to such troubles.

My nurse returned and cooked for us. Old Iguchi and Chōsa joined us and we drank sake together by the fire.

With sake, the teacher's sallow face reddened and he became jolly. He grinned all the time for no reason and I sometimes noticed a flirtatious light in his eyes.

He took a writing brush from his box. Then sucking the end, he showed us a poem, written just as a diversion.

A Poem Presented to Miss Nonaka

I brush away tears as I see you;
You are indeed a worthy child of your father.
How beautiful you are, like Komachi,[15]
How gracefully you move, like a spring breeze.
Like the sun in a mirror you sparkle.
Heaven was there, even in prison.
You were polishing yourself beautifully.
Like a lovely moon, you emerged from murky darkness.

Although he composed this as an immediate amusement, my teacher linked it with a poetic reply he had written during my imprisonment to one of my own works:

I brush away tears as I read your letter;
Worthy of admiration is your blood.
Graceful all your poems, like those of Komachi,
Your knowledge is that of a great scholar.
Like the sun in a mirror you sparkle,
May you continue to triumph.
Light will emerge through the gloom.
Even in prison Heaven will guide you.[16]

Thus he had written about my poems while I was under arrest. Now at last we had met and he had adapted it to describe my appearance and movement. I responded with a smile, but I was a little disturbed and pondered on it.

Although it was a play on words and but a jest, I was

conscious of his eyes as a man. I cannot be anything, except as I am now, with unshaven eyebrows, unblackened teeth and still in long sleeves. I think I must have seemed a very odd forty-year-old woman to him.

Moreover Chōsa, as he grew drunk, started sobbing, saying that he felt sorry to see O-En-sama so young and beautiful and still in long sleeves. I was greatly affected by it. However to hide my embarrassment I burst into laughter.

Then old Iguchi also laughed loudly saying, 'Oh, forgive him. He has grown maudlin since his banishment.'

Late at night, on the way to the porch to bid the teacher farewell, in the darkness in front of the storeroom, my cold hands were covered and held in the teacher's warm grasp. This intimate gesture of love happened in a moment.

At last we had found a day to meet together. I ought to have been content with it. I ought to have been happy.

But in fact I felt weighed down. Why? A vague wretchedness enveloped me.

One day, around that time, when Okamoto Danshichi visited me and said, 'I am gratified to hear that my teacher came to see you', this provided a clue to my misery.

It overlapped somewhere with the slight disturbance I had felt on the first day I had met Danshichi. . . . Yes, that was it. Under house arrest, I had always thought of Master Shinzan as being young, like Danshichi. I could not believe that he had aged since the day I received his first letter, when I was twenty-six. Yet when I first saw him I was embarrassed to find that he reminded me of my eldest brother. I had never imagined him to look so old, for he was two years younger than me. I had been deceived by the involuntary connection with Danshichi.

Having spent half my life under house arrest, I was unaware that life consisted of many conflicts and misunderstandings. I did not know its secrets. I was at a loss in the face of my first experience.

Danshichi was the son of an old retainer in Yamada who had been reduced to the peasantry. He had visited us, with his father, soon after our arrival in Asakura. Danshichi had broad shoulders for his twenty-three years; with his wide forehead and refreshingly manly mien, he did not seem like a young peasant.

On that first day he had stared at me with serious, challenging eyes. He seemed to feel a strong curiosity or sympathy toward me. It was not unpleasant. But a sense of shame sprang up inside me because he was an attractive man, just as I imagined the teacher, whom I had not then seen.

Upon this image I had unwittingly overlaid my idea of the teacher, the only man whom I happened to know. As I had already become acquainted with the young man Danshichi, I was able to understand the emotional connection after I met the teacher. For when I met Danshichi I remember I felt vibrant, as if clouds of spray hung densely around me.

But when I am awake at night in bed, I cover one hand with the other. It reminds me vividly of the skin of a man whom I touched for the first time in my life, the feeling of his palms, rough, bony and warmed by sake.

When I read his letter on 19 November, I realized that he had already decided to resign his office before he had called to see me.

On that morning, unable to bear that I had received no letter for a long time, I sent him one by a messenger. But his letter crossed mine and was delivered soon afterwards. In it he explained that he intended to return to his home in Sue, Yamada, terminating his lectureship for the clan Government.

He wrote that while working for the clan Government

he found, being somewhat brusque and tactless, the seasonal ceremonies and socializing with his senior officers and colleagues were too tiresome for him. He was unable to study as much as he wished and was now resigning his post in order to devote himself to learning and the writing of books at home. Fortunately his lord permitted him to do so.

We have known each other for over twenty years. But he says he is going back to Sue, far away from here, leaving me behind yearning, when I have come to live within two miles of him. Although he was flirting when writing his poem, he had already made up his mind then. What callous behaviour. . . .

I have now learnt something of his theories.

He had studied Suika Shinto under Master Ansai and was subsequently a pupil for ten years by correspondence under Shibukawa Harumi[17], an astronomer for the Edo Government. Being the son of a Shinto priest, he was destined for Shintoism, and after Master Ansai died he was influenced by Lord Kitabatake Chikafusa's Shinto text, *Jin-nō Shōtōki.*[18]

Both Master Ansai and Lord Chikafusa had considered the movements of heavenly bodies in connection with ethics and morality. However, their theories and beliefs about astronomy were so subjective and primitive that Shinzan, upon learning that Shibukawa Harumi had developed his astronomy into an objective experimental science, became an ardent admirer of him.

In astronomy, Shinzan strongly desired to connect Japanese old Shintoism with the movements of heavenly bodies, and to discover the objective, cosmic phenomena by observation and experimentation.

I could understand how Master Shinzan, as Master Harumi's pupil, was so eager to learn, observe and write books, that he gave up his livelihood, his job and his classes. Just as my father zealously spent his life in politics, so the teacher devoted himself to the pursuit of learning.

I understood his excitement, like a rainbow forming a curve towards truth, far away in the sky. My vulgar, earthbound sorrows and agonies were very different from the teacher's excitement. I was so disheartened and lost in thought that I had no desire to talk about his letter to my mother and nurse.

To live, I was ready for any hardship. But in order to realize my eighty-year-old mother's wish for our own house and not to annoy the Iguchis any longer, money was absolutely necessary. Today at last, unwillingly, I wrote asking Lord Kurando for help.

'I would like our new house on the site of the old Magonoshin Mansion, as water is available there.' But there was a more important reason which I could tell no one. I chose the site for its isolation from prying eyes, should the teacher come to see me. How merciless was his letter of today, when I had taken such scrupulous care. My eyes blurred with tears, as I thought I must write him a letter full of resentment.

Following his move to Yamada, I received no letters from him. The shivering cold was growing milder, with the first day of spring approaching.[19] The year, which had been full of activity for me, was drawing to a close.

My personal life became busier and busier, with daily meetings concerning the foundations of the new house and raising money for its construction. Moreover, I had to make medicine for my old mother. In addition, my nurse and I pounded plants in a muller, then pulverized the paste in a mortar to make pilules, which I entrusted to old retainers to sell on our behalf.

Even a tiny amount of savings was gone in almost no time. Today my nurse even had to sell a handsickle. With the money we bought rice which my nurse cooked, and while eating it I joked with her, 'Granny, we can eat a sickle, if we try.' She answered me with a nonchalant air, 'Yes, it tastes quite delicious.'

I feel my heart clad in a tougher skin. Just as a baby's soft skin, if exposed to the cold air, becomes resistant, so the surface of my heart has grown another skin in these last weeks. I was dependent on other people, but now I realize that I am trying to stand on my own feet. The solitude in this world is much severer than that under house arrest, but the severity has a basis in life, to give one power to resist it. This must be living.

I was not always gloomy about the fact that the teacher did not write to me. I sent him letters, one after another, whenever I managed to get a messenger.

In the letters, my first experiences of the amusement and agony of life were expressed freely and wholeheartedly. I was like a child with a new toy. I opened my eyes in wonder to the delicate and complicated changes of everyday life, which surged toward me, flowed around me and ebbed swirling away. I related to him all my feelings and all my anxious efforts to cope. If a messenger was available, I could even manage to send a letter three times a day, a pleasure which I could not have imagined under house arrest.

Usually Danshichi worked for me as a messenger. He came from Yamada to visit me every three days. He was kind enough to collect medicinal herbs and deliver them to me. When I realized this could become the means for my livelihood, I was able to work as an apothecary.

But one day, holding my letter in his hand, with downcast eyes and flushed cheeks, he spoke.

'I am afraid that the teacher asked me, "Are you no longer my pupil, that you are such a frequent messenger for Lady En?" '

Those words contained a bitterness which he could not express clearly. It had not occurred to me that my letters to the teacher were too frequent or that I was being selfish.

Danshichi's blush transferred to my face and the next moment suffused my body.

'Good gracious, has he said so?'

I was barely able to answer him, but I was so embarrassed that I did not know where to put myself.

I felt helpless, as if I would shrivel.

'Do you think so many letters have annoyed him?' I realized that I seemed to be asking his opinion.

'. . . I am sure he was joking.'

His eyes remained downcast and he reddened again as he answered. His eyelids seemed a little swollen and showed something of the stubbornness and refusal of a sulky child.

A sense of danger stirred within each of us. Our feelings were very different but I felt that we were both trying to draw near to each other then.

Later I knew I had been wrong, that I had mistaken this moment.

In truth, living contains many discrepancies and misunderstandings. But I ought not to be disturbed by Danshichi, who is twenty years younger than I. Furthermore, such a young man ought not to be stirred by an old woman like me, I said to myself repeatedly, as if to persuade myself of this.

From then on I felt some hesitation to charge him with my letters to the teacher. I knew already that it was due not to sympathy for Danshichi's position but to my tenderness toward him.

I am sure it was tacitly communicated to Danshichi.

He never failed to ask me, 'Would you by any chance have a letter for him today?'

And he sometimes added, 'Please don't mind what I said.'

Whenever he avoided my gaze or respectfully kept his eyes downcast, I could read the stirring of his heart, although he never expressed it. I knew it now.

One day during that time, when Danshichi brought me one of the teacher's letters, he said, almost to himself, 'The teacher's wife is to have prosperity next year.'

In this region, 'prosperity' means 'to have a baby'. Spontaneously, I exclaimed in astonishment, 'Did she say so? You say "next year", but when next year?'

'I have not been told, but I have observed it. Probably in May,' Danshichi answered, averting his eyes from me.

Just the other day, when I met her I did not notice it, yet even Danshichi, such a young man, was aware of it.

How unobservant! When I thought how unobservant I was, I became aware of Danshichi's masculinity. It was oppressive and I felt like turning my face away. I could not prevent a queer opposition springing up against him. I felt it unforgiveable that he had noticed what I had not seen.

In addition, the teacher's letter on that day greatly discouraged me.

'I would like to call upon you,' he wrote, 'as I am concerned about your mother's condition and the building of your new house. But since there is gossip in the castle town about my previous visit to you, I would prefer not to call at present.'

In surprise I asked Danshichi, 'Well, Danshichi, do you know this too?'

Facing my stern gaze he replied, 'One cannot avoid rumours at any time, wherever one may be.'

'I wonder what the rumour is. Would it be serious enough for the teacher to worry?'

Danshichi did not answer.

'Although I was pardoned,' I muttered to myself, 'I wonder if they mean that ex-detainees should not mix with ordinary people.'

Behind the words lay the pride of a daughter whose father had been an administrator. Although he did not realize that my words were spoken rather arrogantly, he was embarrassed by my tone.

'No, it's not true . . . O-En-sama is too beautiful. That is the reason,' he stammered, as if being forced to say something unpleasant.

Then I remembered the humiliating day when an officer of the clan Government, who had come to see where we were settled, told everybody of how my skin was as youthful as that of a girl of twenty. I remembered how the filthy officer's sticky eyes had crept like a slug all over my body. Danshichi's words reminded me of that earlier humiliation.

'Danshichi, are you baiting me as well?' I shrieked provokingly.

I felt exceedingly angry. However, unlike my anger at the officer's humiliation of me, I was also perplexed to find joy rippling through my heart.

Again Danshichi did not read my mind and he was embarrassed even more. 'Not at all, never . . .' he said, with a flush as far as the nape of his neck and with his head bowed. 'I am very sorry. Please forgive me.'

'All right, say no more. I am stupid enough to be upset by such trifles.'

Then I realized that I had been obsessed with the idea that I was beautiful. 'To be beautiful', which could be most propitious to women, was in my case attended by shame.

Though I had been angered and humiliated by the officer, it had not deeply affected me. On the other hand, I was enveloped more by uneasiness and pain than by humiliation, when the teacher and Danshichi found me beautiful.

In any event, the teacher wrote that he would prefer not to visit me as there was much talk about us. I resisted his idea, as it ill became him to write such a thing.

Under house arrest I never imagined I would hear such vulgar words from him. In those days there had been nothing to estrange me from the teacher. Now an obscure and subtle barrier called 'the world' was standing between us. I disapproved of the fact that such a great man as the teacher regarded the obscure power of the world as an inevitability. It was a great blow to me. And in a subtle way, I was deeply influenced by Danshichi's chance revelation that a baby would be born to the teacher.

A new life created between a man whom I adored and his wife. Upon an ill-fated, childless woman like me, it fell inevitably like a bolt from the blue. I was thrown into a solitary hell. Such a cruel world would never have existed in the house where I used to stay.

'You see, Danshichi, I think I was probably in that house too long, or else I should have stayed there far, far longer. I should have been there till the age of sixty, a very old woman. Anyway I must have come out of the house at an awkward age. Don't you think so?'

Danshichi kept silent. The young, honest and simple man knew at last how meaningless it was to answer frankly such an effusion of feeling. At last he allowed himself to share the same emotion as the daughter of his father's lord, from whom he had previously kept a certain distance.

'. . . Well, don't you think so?. . . . For Master Shinzan, I am nothing in particular. He has to study and write. He has his wife and children. Why does the teacher, who refused to continue his tedious work for the Government, need to choose a friendship with an ex-detainee? It could bring public criticism and expose us to inquisitive eyes. Isn't it quite reasonable that he should not wish to continue it?'

Danshichi still kept silent.

He kept his head bowed like a man suffering torture. It gave me pleasure to know that my words were causing him pain. I felt inclined to be much crueller to him.

'I think he has many things on his mind,' he answered, after a long pause.

'Many things? What do you mean?'

'I am afraid it is beyond my understanding.'

It was not until much later, when disaster struck the teacher, that I became fully aware of those things which Danshichi could now only express indirectly. At this time all I could see was the young man seated before me, suffering my words like torture.

That evening I was standing vacantly on the verandah, with both hands in my sleeves in a slovenly manner, fondling my breasts through the open sides of my kimono.

My breasts, still plump, bouncing and youthful because I was childless and virginal, were nevertheless wearisome to me. Those swellings rose rebelliously with unfulfilled life. The insecurity and fragility of my relationships caused ceaseless turmoil within me. Standing by in vain, watching my flower wither, this seemed the nadir of my life.

It was hard and painful for me to put up with such a moment.

The lingering smell of the millet porridge being slowly cooked by my nurse floated down to the verandah. The motherly smell of the grain made me sadly nostalgic.

Aimlessly I came inside and sat down before the mirror. My face was dimly reflected there. I was harshly gazing at my own familiar features as if they were hateful. Then I tucked up my sleeves and looked at both exposed arms in the glass.

The white skin, always hidden beneath my sleeves, was clear, pale and smooth with fine threadlike blue veins, and quite fresh with a mysterious scent. I felt a sudden urge to injure the moist, silky skin with a blade.

I almost cursed because I could not accept the reason for my youth and beauty. It should not have been so and it was nothing but an evil.

Forty years in confinement had deprived me of everything, of all the happiness I could have attained. Instead it left me with strangely young flesh and an ominously unsettled mind. And now I understand that these were also among the punishments imposed on me.

I am certain that the youth and freshness of a woman with the lifeless and hollow beauty of chastity is more sinister than beautiful. She has no history of being made happy or unhappy by a man, nor has her life been soiled by a man's dirt or his greasy hands, nor injured by his violence.

In order to stop the thought of my abnormal, sinister youthfulness and my hollow beauty, I imposed on it an arrogant idea.

(The teacher is trying to avoid me. He is afraid of me . . .)

I fancied this haughty, arrogant supposition would lessen, even slightly, my present intolerable misery and unhappiness.

The new year arrived. The teacher sent by Danshichi's hand two poems for New Year's Eve and New Year.

At the year end and on New Year's Day I am sure he came up to Kōchi to meet people and exchange greetings, but he did not come to see me.

However, I wrote a poem for New Year to the teacher

and showed it to Danshichi. I entrusted it to him with the following lines:
'I think you have forgotten me and I am a little piqued.'

> *A New Year*
> New Year has fled and Spring is about,
> Man and nature are being renewed.
> Yet warmth has not touched my dwelling,
> The plum has not yet blossomed.

During this year the teacher would be able to realize his cherished desire to go to Edo to study. As our friendship had been stifled by rumour, the teacher's long absence in the far city of Edo might bring a breath of air into my choking heart.

By enduring this separation for a time, I expected that everything would gradually improve. The teacher seemed to have had the same idea as I. In his most recent letter I could detect even by simple remarks that he was missing me.

I had asked him to sell for the highest price to someone with a taste for such things, a sword which my father had treasured and a mirror stand which my father had ordered for my mother in his youth all the way from Nagasaki. In his letter, as he thought it impossible to find a suitable customer in Kōchi, the teacher asked whether it would be better to take them to Ōsaka, Kyōto or Edo, to achieve a higher price.

As it was my dearest wish to see him before he went to Edo, he promised to visit me in the near future.

An unfortunate accident occurred at this important time, so that my reply to his letter, dated 17 February, was lost on the way.

As Danshichi was not due to come and as the other messenger I usually asked was ill, I could find no one to whom I could entrust my letter. Then, happening to learn of a merchant who would conveniently pass by Yamada, I sent my letter to him. I was to blame for my own stupidity. No amount of regret could change it.

'. . . Probably it was opened on the way. You have not written anything which might give rise to scandal, have you? I think it is better to act as if you know nothing for a while . . .' In the teacher's reply, I could tell how anxious and pained he was.

I was upset lest this misfortune bring doubtful rumours and impede the clan Government's granting of permission for his departure. My heart was quivering with the double anxiety.

'. . . In my excitement over your visit to me, I am ashamed to have committed such an irreparable error which allowed the loss of my letter. I most profoundly apologize to you. But since I did not write anything which might give rise to scandal, please dismiss such thoughts. I have now given up the idea that I might meet you.

'I long for you every day and all I can do is to send my love on a cloud.'

In this way, my heartfelt desire to see him was disappointingly thwarted.

If I could have seen him at this time, I would have tried to gain some idea of his anxieties about popular opinion. It seemed in a way that I could not fathom to have some important link with politics.

He was never afraid of acting independently in the cause of learning. He had even taken a firm stand against his teacher. I therefore found it very strange that he was particularly nervous about gossip. This seemed to create the same gloomy, oppressive fear that I had felt during my house arrest, as if rumour was just one aspect of politics.

He intended leaving around 10 March. Although he had been granted permission and was ready to travel, I heard he had a slight fever and postponed his departure. In haste I compounded some medicine for a fever and sent it with a note by Danshichi.

I hear you have a cold. I hope you will recover soon and have a safe journey in fair weather.
Yours sincerely,

On the twelfth, the teacher set sail from Urado Harbour. Of course, I did not go to farewell him. Instead I had a dream.

I had never before seen such a large ship, with so great a spread of canvas. I was on board, my eyebrows shaved, my teeth dyed and dashingly clad in a travelling outfit with hand covers and gaiters. I was looking at the wide sea, raising my sedge hat to one side. Shyly I was saying, 'I have always wanted to visit Edo. How fortunate I am, to be going there as your bride.'

Awakening, I found myself beaming in delight, with a sense of rapture flowing right through my body. And it was this, not the surprise of seeing my face still having eyebrows and white teeth, which made me feel wretched.

I was dejected and chagrined to find that even an irresolute and hollow dream could so easily deceive me and I shed a few tears in the night. Moreover I was to secretly find myself recollecting the momentary hollow dream for comfort, mulling it over and reviewing it with nostalgia.

This self-betrayal and wretchedness meant that when I received a special epistle from the clan lord soon afterwards, I felt deeply insulted.

One part of the epistle stated: 'En, a daughter of the deceased Nonaka Den-emon, is granted a ration for eight persons', while another stated the lord's informal recommendation that I should marry.

As an innocent child everything had been taken away from me by the previous clan lord and for forty years I had languished in that house. Now his successor offered me a ration for eight persons as a very small fief, as a mere particle, no more than a sparrow's tear. I felt humiliated. Even if I must go about begging in rags, or even if I must die of hunger, I would not accept such a benefice.

It was painful even to express my wishes. I smiled nonchalantly and said, 'Why would he grant me a ration when I do not serve him? I have no reason to accept it.' Old Iguchi shed tears and admonished me, without his usual stubborn manner.

'Our most kindhearted lord was appointed from the Shinbashi family in Edo. Although only thirty-three, he is compassionate and understanding. In his respect for Master Shinzan, he engaged him as official Confucianist for the clan Government, and supported his astronomical studies. Moreover, when newly appointed, our clan lord gathered over sixty young samurai in the North Assembly Hall to hear Shinzan give lectures on the history of the Mythological Age from the *Nihon Shoki*.[20] I am sure Master Shinzan's learning could not have become so well established without the good will of the clan lord. And this grant is not so much for you, but for your old mother and nurse.'

This was the first time I had heard of the young and sickly clan lord.

Although I had decided firmly, as an ex-detainee, to avoid politics, I now understood that even the lowest creature, be he ex-detainee or insect, could never escape it.

I decided to accept this meagre grant, this ration for eight persons, because I understood that the only way to avoid politics was to accept that there was no point in withstanding the young, weak clan lord, who was said to be in sympathy with learning. And furthermore, with my old mother and nurse on my hands, I was so poor that we were always short of daily provisions. But my nature repudiated it and I gritted my teeth.

However kind and intelligent the young clan lord may be, he lives in the white, moated castle.

The merciless nature of the castle was unchanged, even by him. If, upon his succession, he had thought of a pardon for us after thirty-seven years under arrest, my youngest brother, who had entered that house at five months, could have seen the world, albeit only for two years. It was not by the will of the merciful clan lord, but by the will of the high, white castle that we were only pardoned when poor Teishirō had died and the Nonaka line had ended. I have never forgiven it. I know I never shall.

It was certainly not his place to advise me to marry one of the old retainers. I was no longer a detainee.

If Master Shinzan had not been away, I would have hastened there in a palanquin and thrown myself in front of him to weep and rail in bitterness.

And if the gatekeeper of the castle had let me pass, I would have strongly rejected this allegedly beneficent young lord's advice to his face.

I am sure he does not know how meaningless it is, or how it may even be hurtful for him to be benevolent. He can never realize that it is also ridiculous. How absurd it is . . .

The old man said that the reason the clan lord advised marriage for me was that he was very reluctant to let the blood of my distinguished father die out.

The old man tried keenly to persuade me, 'If you marry, I am sure you will have a baby. I think it is your bounden duty. If you do not grant his request, I do not think I can make my apologies to my dead master and our clan lord.'

'. . . If I refuse, what will you do?' A smile played about my lips and I arose.

I was physically shocked. I had never considered the possibility of having a baby.

At the same time, I thought my body was still woman enough. Since empty girlhood, my monthly courses had continued on and on, and punished me still, a merciless seal on which was carved the emptiness of my life. The possibility of a fulfilled life, to love a man and to bear a child, was continued vainly over and over in me and carried away in bitterness. It was another penalty.

That physical shock was an admission of my body's power to betray me.

If I decided to agree, I might be able to obtain a part of so-called feminine happiness. I was completely confused.

In the days when I was resigned to thinking that my life would end in detention, in my idle fancies the teacher and I were married.

But when I actually met him, my wishful fantasy turned to a strange demonic one.

It was almost an insult to consider the teacher's poor body, hurt miserably, wracked by poverty, ill-health and meditation since childhood, as that of a man. To my mind he was far from being masculine. As a woman who had long hoped for love, I cherished my own ideal man who was arrogant, critical and uncompromising.

The teacher really was a man in spirit and intellect, but the feminine side of me could never disregard a man's body, and I already saw this in young Danshichi. The man whom I embraced in the demonic daydream was not in fact the teacher, but resembled Danshichi. In Master Shinzan, I did not see a man's body. In Danshichi, I did not see a great mind. Although I had had little opportunity to awaken, now, through the unexpected interference of a young, kind lord, I was offered the chance to bear a child in a cruel union with some old retainer whom I had never seen.

The pardon allowed me to grasp my own destiny. If I could bear it I could choose my life. I could become a wife and thereby a mother, for which every woman yearns with inexplicable longing from childhood.

Once I was punished for the blood of my father. Now I am offered marriage because of this selfsame blood. I wonder how I can be blessed with woman's conjugal happiness just because those in power order it. If it is allowed as compensation for the forty years I bore under house arrest, I shall say that I want my teacher's hardy spirit and Danshichi's young, sturdy body. I shall say I want both. As men have several concubines, I shall say I want two men – I remember Princess Sen-hime.[21] If I had the power . . .

But however freely I might imagine, the hard fact is that I am only a poor powerless maiden, an ex-detainee. I am only an old woman over forty.

I was determined that while I was still woman enough, I would strangle my womanhood with my own hands.

With three kilograms of silver from Lord Kurando, together with money I raised from everything I could sell and with the assistance of Danshichi's father, Okamoto, and other old retainers, a small humble house was built and I was able to move by the end of March.

It was at the foot of the hill, commanding a view of the forest of Konomaru Shrine. Behind the house was a beautiful bamboo thicket leading to a wood at the base of the mountain. A clear stream ran through the thicket and alongside the garden down towards the main road.

Danshichi channelled the water into a bamboo pipe, through which it fell into a big jar, making a loud, festive noise. The overflowing water then filled a small pond in the garden and flowed on again through the water grasses down into the stream.

Except for the people who came to collect medicine and an occasional sick person, nobody visited. The solitary house, protected by the bamboo thicket, was quiet in the spring.

> In the evening of an April day in Asakura
> Mountains are green, fields are full of flowers.
> This small grass-roofed house, with its brushwood fence shutting out the sun,
> Refuses the Spring and is dark.
> My brothers float on my tears as my eyes brim over
> I think of my father and mother as well,
> Sadly trying not to recollect a man whom I love,
> I amuse myself with butterflies.

I mixed medicines every day, in order to make pilules. I named them Ekkiku-maru and entrusted them to old retainers to sell for me on their peddling tours.

By ones and twos, people came to take my medical advice, paying with a little money or some rice or vegetables. In this manner I managed to make a small living.

It was 2 July, in midsummer, when my teacher returned.

This time too, I made no attempt to welcome him or to call upon him. Four months parting had been very long. But I could not fathom how this or how his concern for popular opinion might affect our relationship.

When Danshichi came to tell me that a meeting was to be held, for eager pupils to listen to a lecture by the teacher and to greet him after his absence, I agreed, after some hesitation, to attend. For the first time, I travelled the seven mile distance in a palanquin to Danshichi's house in Yamada.

The palanquin was carried at a run alongside the Funairi Canal, created by my father. Edged with water grasses, the canal flowed abundantly through the wide green rice fields and innocently reflected the peace and quiet of an eve in midsummer.

When I arrived at the Okamotos, it was night. The brightly lit front parlour was filled with men. The lecture had already started and I slipped in at the back, unobserved, near the edge of the verandah. For the first time I listened to his lecture on *The Great Learning*.[22]

Browned by the sun, the teacher seemed healthier than before. He looked serious with his piercing eyes, unlike the last time I had met him. At a glance I realized that those four months had been of great significance for him. His still-thin, poor body glowed with inner life and seemed to convey increased authority and an immovable strength.

I understood that a new, indefinable quality had been born and was growing in him. This new quality might not draw me to him, rather it might drive me away. In fact, later I knew it was exactly so. But I was fascinated then by the strength which shone from within him.

The people around me faded from my awareness. I was face to face only with him. This was the man I had longed for, over twenty years. My sole desire was this happiness. Our bond was as close as any between man and woman. I said to myself that I must keep this bond and this happiness.

After the lecture, the front parlour was turned into a dining room. Danshichi's mother was sensible enough to permit me to remain on the cool back verandah. I reclined and listened to the commotion of young men's spirited voices which burst forth from the front parlour.

It was enjoyable to be alone.

'Lady En, here you are.'

Suddenly the teacher was beside me. Tucking the sleeve of his hemp summer kimono up on his shoulder, he squatted down, looking at the dark garden.

'I have been thinking I must tell you . . .' he said, and mentioned the clan lord's advice to me during his absence.

'I originally asked this of the clan lord. I must apologize to you as I hear you are very angry.'

In a low voice he let the words fall. It was so unexpected that I could not utter a sound.

Still looking toward the dark garden, he repeated, 'If you are angry, I can only apologize to you. But I regret it still that your father's blood will die out.'

'If I heard it from somebody else, I could have borne it. I never imagined, even in a dream, that I would hear it from you directly. I feel much bitterness towards you.'

Without noticing, I edged closer to him as he was looking at the dark garden.

But the teacher was silent and remained squatting, facing the garden. In his demeanour I suddenly sensed his masculinity.

I was dimly aware of his complex state of mind and of many things obscurely mingled: a man who has the effrontery to trick and conspire, quite unlike young Danshichi; the possibility that even a merciless and cruel man might be considerate; something like the wariness of a man sullied by the dirt of living; a man who can rashly stake his life on a risky scheme; a man who seems to be frightened of the world but who, on the contrary, actually has the audacity to manipulate the world.

He used the desire for continuing my father's line to conceal his pity for my lonely, fragile womanhood. I was seated, stifling the urge to cry and throw myself at his knees, while the voices of young people in the parlour asked for the teacher.

I was trying to believe his love then, there being a love which can only be expressed in such a form.

That moment was a turning point in my life; doubtful and ignorant of the world, and apt to be shaken by even trifling matters, I achieved a bitter and hard rebirth that night.

Just as a moth must first cast off its skin before it can fly freely alone, so too I laboured to slough off a piece of skin from my heart.

In the autumn, my mother died. The teacher came with Danshichi for a ceremony and to keep vigil and we talked through the night.

Since he had returned from Edo he was much busier with his studies, exchanging letters with the scholars Shibukawa Harumi, Kaibara Ekken, and others. He had given no lecture since then, nor had I had an opportunity to see him.

After bidding a last farewell to my mother, my daily life became much freer with only two of us, me and the placid nurse, permitting me time to indulge in reading a book as my fancy dictated, while still seeing poor patients and giving them medicine generously.

I went out only at night.

I would go out, covering my face and head completely with a purple hood, putting on my brother's riding habit and wearing my father's short sword at my side.

The field path was filled with noisy autumn insects, which continued their singing despite my quiet footsteps. The insects, heedless of danger, performed as if this moment was the climax of their lives, their incessant rich noise filling the field. It was fitting for me to love the loneliness of this pitiful grand performance, for loneliness ate into my soul as I went through the night field in men's clothes.

One day, at the beginning of the next year, in a letter, Master Shinzan reprimanded and criticized me for walking out in male attire, for my haughtiness in not using titles for the important clan officials in conversation, and for the frequent visits of young Danshichi.

'How kind of you to chide and instruct me for my faults. I am indeed grateful to you. I will try to follow your advice, in spite of my poor ability. However, one way or another, I may fail you because, as Chu Hsi says, a woman's uprightness is drained away by love.'

Although all his words meant much to me, I would neither grant the important clan officials the least title, nor give up the idea of walking about alone at night, and I would not consider telling Danshichi to moderate his frequent visits to me.

My reprimand from the teacher revived a familiar, sweet sensation. I thought I perceived another form of his love, which I had discovered unexpectedly on the night of his lecture at the Okamotos.

But it would neither affect nor change my way of life. Though I might be a delicate moth floating in the dirty world, I could fly on my own wings.

I was rather concerned lest other, groundless, rumours reach the ears of Danshichi and his father, and thereby prevent Danshichi from coming to see me.

Talk of my behaviour, for which the teacher had censured me, could not have failed to reach their ears. I thought that Danshichi, who had acted as if he knew nothing, must know of it.

One day he suddenly said, 'O-En-sama, any gossip you might hear, please do not be disturbed . . .'

For a moment I held my breath, taken aback by his resolute attitude but I answered unconcernedly, 'Why, I shall never get angry about false rumours. It must be bitter for you . . .'

Instantly he reddened around his hairline.

'. . . Your words are more than I deserve. I am an unworthy peasant. I would never dream of it being onerous. If you allow me, I want to serve you all my life.'

Danshichi raised his eyes to me.

There was something significant in his look and I lowered my gaze in spite of myself. Although his eyes were shining with a sincere, true devotion, I could not but fear him then.

I was afraid of this simple peasant, who was like a panting young animal of the plains with his powerful, crude longing and his strong, healthy odour.

My fear seemed instantly to be communicated to Danshichi and his complexion changed slightly. Averting his eyes, he said, 'I am very sorry to have been impolite. I am afraid I must excuse myself today,' and rose to his feet.

When he visited me four days later, Danshichi was as faithful as usual and as diligent as if nothing had happened. Without being ordered, he found tasks to perform.

Before I was aware he had learned his place in my household.

In this way, I seemed at long last to be growing into a woman, a mature human being.

– 5 –

LAMENT

Today, after a modest ceremony for the fiftieth anniversary of my father's death, my heart was gladdened by an unexpected letter from the teacher.

> It was so unusual to receive a letter from you that I immediately left my work and engrossed myself in it. As you mentioned, it is the fiftieth anniversary of my father's death. I held a humble service for the dead with just a few white-haired old retainers, for, as you well know my father's nature, it was hardly necessary to invite any officials.
>
> I am sure you will understand when I say that my memories of my youth long ago are so full of my brothers that I am sometimes too sad to sleep.
>
> Although people visit me in my rural life, I cannot really say that I have friends. I have not been to the castle town in the last few years as all my days are spent in compounding medicine and making pilules. Sadly this year is drawing to a close.
>
> I spend every day thinking about you and wishing I could see you.
>
> Yours sincerely,
>
> 26 December,
> 1712, the second year of Shōtoku

It is already six years since I was last able to see the teacher. In recent years we have rarely corresponded and I have kept my distance from him.

The teacher's laborious work. *The Main Shrines of Tosa* was completed in March, six years ago. The following month he went up to Kyōto to have it inspected by the Yoshida family, who were responsible for shrines throughout the country.

The fifth clan lord, Toyofusa, one of the teacher's few friends, had long been ill in bed and had been waiting for his return. Although the lord was delighted to greet the teacher when he returned from Kyōto on 17 May, he was dead less than three weeks later, at the young age of thirty-five.

The dreamy, weak clan lord left behind no children, only his favourite celestial globe which he had used each night to observe the constellations.

Without a guardian of the castle, misfortune was inevitable and could occur at any time.

Amidst some ill feeling, the fifth clan lord had been appointed to his position from the Shinbashi, a branch family of the Tokugawa, as his predecessor had also been childless. In his place, his younger brother, Toyotaka, was compelled to inherit the Shinbashi title and upon Toyofusa's death, this younger brother was promoted to become the sixth clan lord, supported by relatives of the Tokugawa. In this way the Shinbashi fief fell vacant, ripe for seizure by the Edo Government.

Shurinosuke, the younger brother of the first clan lord, Kazutoyo, had two sons who served different families. Dewa, the third son, was adopted by the Fukao family, chief retainers of the Tosa clan, and his descendant Wakasa was the present head. The fourth son, Kazutada, was given a fiefdom and appointed head of the Shinbashi for his services to the Tokugawa Government.

When Toyofusa succeeded as fifth clan lord of Tosa, Wakasa was discontented, thinking that he should have been chosen, according to seniority. It is said that it did not emerge at the time, but when Lord Toyofusa died and Tosa was simply notified that Lord Toyotaka of the Shinbashi had been appointed, Fukao Wakasa was furious.

He and his sons had such a passion for learning that the teacher had been lecturing them in their own home. Wakasa consulted Master Shinzan as to whether the elder or younger son should succeed as governor, and was told that it would be reasonable for the elder to take precedence.

Lord Toyotaka's succession to the Tosa clan was discussed all over the province as being against the principle of seniority. Sengoku Idayū, a chief superintendent for the Tosa clan warriors, who was an enthusiastic admirer of Master Shinzan and one of his pupils, led the vanguard of counter-attack.

But the relatives of the Tokugawa who favoured Lord Toyotaka, were supported by the members of the Shōgun's Council of Elders and they justified themselves by claiming it as the will of the dead Lord Toyofusa.

This plan by the relatives of the Tokugawa, to seize the Shinbashi's fief and thereby abolish the family, accorded with the Edo Government's intention.

Of course it is a sealed book to me why it was desirable for the Tokugawa relatives to abolish the Shinbashi. It could simply be said that they had long planned it, since they had sent the young, weak Lord Toyofusa to Tosa as its fifth governor. And nobody knows how far he himself had desired the title.

The dreamy Lord Toyofusa might have known it and

pretended not to – I could imagine the loneliness and resignation of this sickly, benevolent man.

On 7 August the new governor, Lord Toyotaka, came to Tosa and soon reprisals began against the people who had opposed his succession.

First of all the chief superintendent Sengoku Idayū was placed under house arrest. Second Fukao Wakasa was ordered to be detained in his residence and to transfer the headship to his son, to prevent the family being deprived of its estate.

Some of the furious retainers took the strong view that they should all bravely seek voluntary exile. But Wakasa was intelligent, so he obeyed the order, choosing to keep his land rather than freedom.

I watched the reform coldly, from far outside the circle.

Everything seemed absurd and I took no heed of how it would end. The same destiny which had visited my grandfather now fell upon Fukao Wakasa, a descendant of Shurinosuke who had triumphed against my grandfather long ago.

The chief retainer Wakasa was a grandson of Fukao Dewa who had driven us into forty years house arrest. His family had been guardians to the clan lords and had exercised power since Shurinosuke's time. Now several others in authority regarded it as the best time to undermine his influence.

Now, as in the old times, men crowd round politics and power and the vortex of hatred forms history.

Being no more than a scholar, how could the teacher possibly live outside the whirlpool? Many years before, even I as a mere child of four, had been worthy of hatred. I was foolish enough to think that Master Shinzan, Wakasa's mentor and adviser, might have been able to live outside the swirl of hatred.

Later I learnt that as well as these incidents, others

gradually accumulated from long ago, had contributed to the hatred against him.

Throughout this time the superintendents of the clan Government were ordered to spy on the teacher's daily activities.

I heard about it from Lord Kurando.

> Regarding Tani Tanzaburō:
>
> During the time of the former clan lord, this man maintained a special friendship with Wakasa and Idayū. Recently moreover, he lodged at Wakasa's house in Sagawa and while up in the castle town, he called upon Idayū every night.
>
> There was evidence that he held a secret discussion with Wakasa in Sagawa to the effect that as soon as the new governor should return to Tosa from his alternate attendance in Edo, they would write refusing to accept him. Knowing the impossibility of this demand, they would then deny his right of succession, although it would lead to the extinction of their lines.

The mission was reported in February with several other false accusations. And again in March.

> Regarding Tani Tanzaburō:
>
> This man has stayed for several days in Sagawa. In addition he has often called upon and held secret talks with Sengoku Idayū who is living modestly as ordered. Tanzaburō is known far and wide, and we are forced to admit that he has great literary ability. People cannot read his character, but still find him very plausible.

Again in April, there was a report to the clan Government:

> Regarding Tani Tanzaburō's behaviour and ideas:
> He is said by many to be cunning and our investigation has proved it. We cannot but acknowledge how ingeniously he won the hearts of men under him. All who know him, including his pupils and friends, speak of his wisdom. By aligning himself with them, he cleverly arouses public opinion to achieve sympathy and curries favour with those in power. As he is familiar with astronomy, the accurate predictions of this religious hypocrite are used to confound and frighten people. His intelligence permits him to deceive the public that much better. It is said that he might obstruct government policy.

Everybody, the public and officials, had too high an opinion of the teacher. 'How crafty, tricky and ambitious he seemed in the reports,' I said to my nurse and Danshichi with a cold smile.

It seems that they feared his achievements; his controversial theories and his astronomical observations were viewed as almost akin to the magical practices of a Bateren.[23]

When mutual understanding dies out, is it inevitable for people to hate and fear one another? . . . . He had been so timid in opposing the world . . .

'He is still very plausible,'. . . . what does that mean?

It was clear to me now that his position as a scholar had always been less secure than I had imagined, except during the term of the young, weak clan lord. Even in his youth, during our house arrest, he had written to us that he was sometimes censured by the law for his speech and behaviour.

The clan Government's hatred of the teacher seemed to go back to the time when scholars were banished after my father lost his position. Then the clan Government had provoked the derision of discerning men throughout the country by banishing almost all the scholars whom my father had supported.

Later when peace reigned over the land, every clan competed for the best scholars to raise the standard of talented men to the highest degree, in order to assure their future prosperity. To recover their damaged reputation, the Tosa clan Government tried to send its young samurai to one Ogata Sōtetsu[24] in Kyōto, who received the high allowance of 300 Koku.

About the same time Master Shinzan had just started shining as a Confucianist. Young men in Tosa eagerly sought to attend his lectures and showed no interest in having Sōtetsu as a teacher.

Because it had lost face over this issue, the hatred of the clan Government had touched the teacher for the first time. But not until many years later was there a chance for the longstanding hatred to take shape.

Although it seemed to me that disaster fell upon him suddenly, it was not actually so. Probably it was not entirely unexpected and he may have always been prepared for such misfortune to befall him.

Otherwise we cannot survive for even a day in this world, of that I am sure.

On 6 May the teacher received a messenger, ordering him to keep to his house in Sue.

> Regarding Tani Tanzaburo,
> Details are as follows:
> It is forbidden for you to go out of doors; you are confined to your house. As it is a minor crime, you are permitted to keep your hair long and leave your forehead shaven. But you are forbidden to engage in teaching or to accept visitors.

I heard about it two days later.

'Although I felt I must tell you within the day, I had a fever and a swollen throat and I could not come earlier. I am very sorry.'

Danshichi was still unwell, with a drained face and a white cloth bound around his neck as a compress. Silently, I was gazing at his shaven forehead, blanched as a sheet of paper.

Once I was imprisoned and the teacher was in the outer world. Now I am out and he is confined.

Suddenly I felt a strong drumming noise in my ears. It pierced my skull and went away. After that, I felt myself slip from my body as if cast out somewhere on a vast, silent moor.

I stood up in a daze. Without speaking, I walked around behind the kneeling Danshichi; I laid my hand gently on his forehead and without thinking I took his temperature in order to prescribe some medicine.

Danshichi did not expect that. In surprise he moved a little and his ear-lobes reddened. I noticed them, but I felt nothing.

His broad forehead was slightly sweaty with fever, and conveyed intense emotion. In spite of his fever he had dared to come to me with such tragic news, and the only thing I could do for him was to make up a remedy.

After the teacher submitted to the order, his pupils were forced to study under Ogata Sōtetsu. Initially, his best pupil Miyaji Shōshichirō was sent to Kyōto and later several others were ordered to follow him. But the following spring, they returned together from Kyōto. Shōshichirō presented the written petition:

'Last year, I went to Kyōto to study under Ogata Sōtetsu. However I disagree with his theory and therefore I would like to resign my service. I wish you to rescind my allowance.'

Iguchi Chōsaemon told me, 'I hear all the other

samurai followed him with the same request. The prestige of the Government was utterly destroyed.'

Since Chōsa looked gloomy and sad whenever I saw him and usually seemed to keep out of my way, I was surprised that he visited me with this news.

'Do you think that perhaps they will be treated even more harshly now?' I asked him on the verandah, as I poured out tea for him.

'However harshly the Government might punish them, it cannot change man's mind.'

Chōsa stubbornly and gloomily curled his lips with a cold smile.

I averted my eyes quietly. I was greatly impressed by his lifelong loyalty for us. Although I felt affection for old Iguchi, in my heart I could find no warmth for Chōsa. Deep within me, I feared and hated this gloomy man, as if there were some part of him that I could not bear to see.

In the summer, in August, the punishment I had dreaded was inflicted on the teacher's young pupils.

The heaviest penalty was imposed on Shōshichirō, that he must leave the castle town and be confined to Usanoura.

As the teacher considered Shōshichirō to be the most promising among his pupils, he was deeply perturbed by the news and paced about his room, heaving deep sighs.

'I hear', said Danshichi, 'he was very agitated and could not eat. He sat up all night blankly, gulping down sobs.'

And he added, 'Shōshichirō's only relative is his mother. It must be unbearable for the teacher to think of that mother's heartbreak.'

I listened in silence to the unhappiness which stormed around the teacher, just as I listen to a cold wintry blast outdoors when, on my thin knees, I work the mortar, making medicines.

This is my tenth year of freedom. This is the actual state of the free world, the outer world for which I yearned so greatly.

Under house arrest, I used to be anxious to see politics at first hand. Now I am amidst politics. Now I am in the raging storm.

I feel a deep abhorrence of the tragedy. I believe it is all brought about by foolishness, which is the reason I find it so abominable. And yet, it is repeated incessantly in the name of politics.

Yesterday, 11 October, was a festival for the Nonaka House for the Dead. Almost all my family had died, but even the dead need a small house to live in, much more so my brothers who ended their lives in exile.

This six foot square humble shrine for the dead had been built near the house of the Komaki family in Yamada. The shrine and its plot had been purchased with the money from my father's sword and my mother's mirror, which the teacher had sold years before in Ōsaka.

This was the paternal home of Komaki Jirohachi who had followed my father young to the grave. I had placed his mortuary tablet as a guest in this House for the Dead. I had put some small personal objects in an oblong chest as an offering to them.

All the inhabitants of this house, except my father, had been born only to die. They were pitiful people, being expected to die, and awaiting each other's deaths as if this was their only aim. I am relieved that the dead are peaceful, neatly placed in this lovely, small House for the Dead.

I did not build this shrine for sutra chanting or prayers to Buddha. The dead had been within me until they had this small house in which to rest. The festival was for my dead loved ones and for me. Filthy Shinto priests and monks were not needed.

Every year I read out to the dead a memorial address which I had written. Although I was growing old, I looked just as they had known me, with eyebrows, with unblackened teeth and still in a long sleeved kimono.

One day I will join them in this lovely small shrine. I would like the Komaki family to hold the festival for me then. I would like them to speak to me in the same way.

> Every year on 11 October, celebrate with glutinous, steamed rice with red beans and tasty sake. Never desecrate it by false accusations against these pure souls. Never ask monks or nuns to take the service. Celebrate the festival with the Komakis's descendants as leaders.
>
> Today I respectfully offer the rice and sake to your spirits. In this beautiful country scenery, I cherish all my memories of you.

It is already the seventh year of the celebrations. Since the day before yesterday I have been staying with the Komakis. The Komakis' eldest son has just wed and in the house the helping women are noisily splashing water in the kitchen. I hear them pound rice for cake and serve it out for the new couple. In this way, whatever misfortune may bluster around, people still try to find some small personal happiness in order to carry on their lives.

I strolled out through the field to Nakano to my father's cottage, where he had died.

This year, we had been blessed with such good weather that a luxuriant autumn crop covered the plain of Kagamino, created by my father. It spread far and wide, filled after decades with the gentleness of man's touch. The air was clear and crisp, with a lovely odour of ripened grain. The blue wild daisies were in full bloom in the field, as if reflecting the colour of the clear sky. Being so near the teacher's house in Sue, I felt light-hearted enough to send a letter to him by messenger this morning.

'Having come to Yamada, it amuses me to find that even the colour of the flowers varies from place to place. The blue of the wild daisies is so bright and lovely that I trust you will take pleasure in the one here plucked for you. The older I grow, the less enjoyable life becomes, except for reading, mornings and evenings. Yet life is still worthwhile. I beg you to take care of yourself.'

While writing, 'Yet life is still worthwhile,' I remembered that in letters he had sent me in confinement such words as 'While there is Heaven, there is life' or 'Heaven will guide you, even in prison' had consoled me.

Yet now, although I used the same ideas in my letter. I did not believe them. What is 'Heaven'? What is it we call 'life'? Now I think that man creates his own life.

Today too, the abundant water of the Funairi Canal flowed quietly between the water grasses, and the boats, laden almost to water level with their piled up cargoes of rice ears, plied to and fro. I plucked autumn flowers, burnet and scabious, on my way, to offer at a small shrine which had been built on the site of my father's retreat.

Coming up to an earthen bridge, I remembered I had met the teacher's wife unexpectedly there when I had visited Yamada for the previous year's celebration.

That had also been a serene, balmy, spring-like day. Holding a large bundle in her arms, she had said she was on her way to deliver a home-sewn kimono. We stood and talked for a while, with the odour of the ripened rice ears floating on the dry autumn air.

It was already over eight years since the teacher had been confined to his house. I imagined their hard life, supported by the limited means of this woman. During these few years, three of the teacher's sons had died, one after another. I was saddened by their unhappiness, so similar to my own feeling over the pointless deaths of all my brothers.

For a while I stood, watching her depart. Her sturdy shoulders showed the will power of a woman who supported all her family. I wondered if she was a woman who had happily devoted herself to a husband who had sacrificed his whole life to learning.

Her stance indicated her practical attitude to life. I clearly understood that I could never experience it. Even if I could peep into her life, the many strands of happiness and sorrow which, with children and husband, had created her immovable strength, seemed too grave and immense for one freed at forty-three.

I did not envy her, nor did I wish to eulogize her, but I felt her to be great and courageous.

As I was walking in the field in the gleaming late afternoon sun, I felt the dry wind blow against my sleeves.

The canal, the field, and even the steady breeze are no different from that day a year ago. The rows of golden rice ears farther ahead seem to be rippling a little in the setting sun. Sometimes, from where I stood, I could see the Funairi sparkling beyond the gently waving grain.

A letter from the teacher had arrived when I came back to the Komakis.

'I have completed a considerable part of my writings. I think I have finished half of what I intended. But I now feel, having reached this far, that it does not seem worth showing to anyone except my son. It might be sufficient as a guide for him. If he is endowed with more ability than I, he could extend this work beyond my knowledge.'

He was bemoaning how little he could pursue thoroughly in his lifetime. I read it over and over, for unexpectedly, it sobered me greatly, like reading a last testament. And since his stomach ailment was worsening, I was secretly concerned for him.

Although my nurse was bowed with years, she was never ill and worked hard, pounding plants in the muller and pulverizing the paste in a mortar to make pilules. Between my nurse and I there had developed a much greater harmony than that between a mother and her daughter or between sisters. I never doubted that we felt as one, and I took it for granted that she would be with me as long as I lived.

It was during one night at the beginning of October the following year that my beloved nurse died suddenly from a slight illness. In the morning, she lay down on her bed, saying that she had a touch of a cold. It saddened me to see my nurse lying still, with a thin quilt on her, so old and small like a bagworm[25] in the late autumn.

I made some medicine for her, gave her some starch gruel and laid my bed beside hers.

All evening I read *The Tale of Genji*, and it was after midnight when I fell asleep. When I glanced at her, her breathing was soft and heavy.

But in the morning, when I awoke and straight away looked at her, already an indescribable, enormous silence, visible only as death, had shrouded her small body.

The quiet way she met her death without troubling anyone, as if to show she cared for me until her end, was typical of her manner. My eyes were full of tears of sorrow for her. She had not wished to bother me by asking me to take her hand at the last moment. Left behind, it made me so much lonelier.

My nurse, widowed young, had fed me her own milk and entered the house with us when the Nonakas were exiled.

My eldest brother could not bear the tragedy of the young nurse pining away in our place of exile and tried to force her to leave the house and to marry, but she would not listen to him, I hear. She was lively and carefree by nature but she had a strong will and never deferred to anyone, once she was so resolved.

'I have had a good life. You must not mourn at all, O-En-sama.'

Holding her small body, still slightly warm, I felt as if she would speak to me at any moment.

I was now all alone. Nothing broke the silence but the water through the pipe and nothing moved but Tama, the cat.

In the daytime, I kept inside, with the brushwood door closed, and did nothing but read melancholy tales, while at night I went out walking, with my head covered by a purple hood.

Each house in the village had a bamboo bush behind and a white-blossomed plum tree in front. Winter, with its frozen river path and ice crystals breaking through the ground, had come to an end. Every night, whether moonlit or dark, the plum flowers cast their perfume over the village.

My poor patients were lying in those houses. They naturally came to regard all the medicines and treatments I prepared for them as an alms giving. The peasants were all poor, cunning and impudent, but on the other hand they admired me candidly.

While the peasants accepted that as the daughter of a harsh ex-administrator, I could never be on their side, they nevertheless acknowledged that I was a pitiful woman, unheeded by the world and they welcomed me to sit with them in a contented circle.

Being an odd, strange maiden with eyebrows and unblackened teeth, they willingly allowed me in to sit by their fireside. The unwitting contempt and pity of the peasants towards me became the way they shared their friendship.

I well knew their accuracy and astuteness in judging other people, and how crafty and impertinent they were. And I liked the innate good sense with which they accepted their lowly status.

For their contented circle, they had only a blazing fire and plenty of coarse tea. Those old peasants' faces took on the blazing colour of the beautiful bright, flickering firelight. I could read each peasant's life as I looked at every line on his old face. I enjoyed spending evenings with them and listening to their talk.

In this way, the seasons change and life continues.

Master Shinzan's confinement had already entered its twelfth year. As usual, at the end of the old year, Danshichi brought me his poems for New Year's Eve and New Year's Day.

The Last Day of the Year of the Cockerel
Eleven years have passed, though I am not yet free.
Year after year I am turning white, distilling the knowledge of scholars.
Many ideas occupy me, though it is the winter of my life.
It is my destiny to watch the day pass.

The First Day of the Year of the Dog
I see the twelfth year in, still without my freedom.
Year after year, nothing much happens, here far from the castle town.
What joy it is to read the treasures of scholars.
I turn my tranquil face to the wind.[26]

I was hoping for a notification of his release on New Year's Day, but in vain,

The purple vetch was in full bloom, carpeting the fields around my house. From the mountain behind the cedar pollen could be seen floating on the east wind, making the air hazy and fragrantly sweet, day and night.

In my garden, the golden mallow roses[27] blossomed, their heads drooping heavily. Near there, even after dark, a dim flowery light remained. Every autumn, Danshichi cut new bamboos to replace the old water pipe, and in spring he swept the watercourse and cleaned out the fallen leaves which had sunk to the bottom of the small pond.

This year, he visited me, bringing heavy blooms of cut peonies. He placed the large white and purple flowers in the pot of Odo-Ware,[27] so loved by my father, and put it in an alcove.

Spring passed and summer came. On 1 June the teacher received notification that he was permitted to walk freely around his district, although he was still classified as an offender.

Naturally, I was so delighted that tears sprang to my eyes. But I simply sent him a congratulatory letter, as I had no intention of seeing him. For Kōchi was far beyond his permitted boundary and Asakura, where I lived, was that much farther. If I should visit him while he was still regarded as an offender, it would quite obviously cause trouble for him.

In October, I was due to go to Yamada for the annual ceremony, then it would be possible to see him without attracting attention.

Nobody will be able to hide the teacher from me any more. I prepare myself for the prospect of certain happiness. I am joyful with anticipation. It represents the greatest luxury I can possess. So I imagine. Yet perhaps I am deceiving myself by daring to hope. Something makes me hesitate to see him again, nay, some fear springs within me that I will feel emptiness when I meet him.

But while I was still hesitating, at the end of July, the teacher suddenly died.

When Danshichi came running out of breath to tell me, I was at my daily work pounding the muller. I was dumbfounded and my body trembled. Unthinkingly, I grabbed his arm roughly. Glassy-eyed, I continued to tremble violently.

I was stunned. Every day, the summer sun rose and set. The world seemed to be moving by as if nothing had happened.

Unaware of the length of the days or the hot weather, I felt only the dazzle of the sun. Heaven and earth seemed gleaming white, like a strange world where all sound had died.

In the dusky room, all day long I sat with my hands folded on my knees. I neither meditated nor thought of anything in particular.

When night came, I would lie dozing like a beggar, and lethargically find sunshine upon me in the morning. Whenever I looked outdoors, where the summer sun blazed away, I narrowed my eyes like an owl or a blind man, unable to bear the dazzle. I felt that I could never again go out into that sunshine.

My body was constantly drained of will and an immense emptiness spread within me. Although Danshichi visited me in great concern, I was heavy hearted. At this time, I had rather be left quite alone.

I was informed by Danshichi that Miyaji Shōshichirō, who had already been under house arrest in Usanoura for eight years, and had only communicated with the teacher by letter, could not bear to stay in this province now that the teacher had died, and had applied to the Government for permission to leave the clan. At the beginning of August, this was granted and he went up to Kyōto.

And in December, Kakimori, the only surviving child of the teacher, also went up to Kyōto, leaving Tosa behind. For the teacher had died while still an offender, so the clan Government did not allow his son to inherit.

Everyone had gone. I tried to smile, as I thought of the young people who could flee somewhere else to find a future. But my wasted cheek and dry lips refused to smile.

I shall not go anywhere. There is no place for me to flee. Nay, I myself am now in another country. Wherever I may be, I am nothing but a stranger in a far country. No matter how politics may crowd, swirl and rage around me, I am concerned with nothing any longer. I am completely estranged from everyone and everything.

I am utterly destroyed, and no man's sympathy can warm me. I am more an object than a human being.

I spent the days by keeping to my room, where I untied letters sent by the teacher, repeatedly re-read each one and remembered my replies.

All I could read now were the letters which he had left behind. Not one word of the voluminous writings on which he spent his life, including those from the twelve years of his confinement, saw the light of day.

The teacher had forbidden his son to remove his books from the house after his death.

'My father imagined that another disaster might fall upon my mother and me if they were printed', Kakimori had said, laughing.

I closed my door to everyone, threw aside my pill-making and sat face to face with the teacher in the dusky room all day long. I talked endlessly with him. The teacher returned again, solely for me. Just as long ago, I had been in detention, now I was sitting with the teacher, just the two of us, in this prison with the brushwood door shut.

Now I knew that I had merely come out of one prison and moved into another.

Days, months and years pass mercilessly, even in here.

1719, the fourth year of Kyōhō, opened and drew to a close.

I ground plants in the muller, pulverized the paste and continued to make a living as before. Occasionally I would walk out at night in men's clothes. But nothing moved me any longer, and I rarely thought about the day or season.

Even when I joined the poor peasants around the fireside, I felt far away from them, like a foreigner. With bright firelight thrown on all the faces, I seemed to be sitting in a glowing circle of flame. Their gruff voices seemed far, far away and very low, so that I could barely hear them. It was as if they spoke a strange tongue and I made no attempt to follow them.

The fifth year of Kyōhō began, and drew to a close.

In the sixth year of Kyōhō, from far Sukumo in Hakata, a letter was sent to tell me of the death of Shōjo, my young sister. I read it without emotion, shedding not even a tear, and folded it with care.

I have been nineteen years out of prison and here too the dead have piled up like leaves around me. I have now reached sixty-one, and I remain here alone. I shall continue to do so.

NOTES

1 Chu Hsi (1130–1200 AD) was a Neo-Confucianist Chinese philosopher whose works became popular in seventeenth-century Japan.
2 *Koku*. Income was measured in annual rice yield. One Koku equals approximately five bushels. It was calculated as the amount of rice necessary to feed one person for one year.
3 *Chuyoshoku: Commentary on the Doctrine of the Golden Mean* by Chu Hsi.
4 Translated by Dr I.J. McMullen, with reference to James Legge's translation of *The Doctrine of the Mean*.
5 *Kana*. The Japanese syllabary of abbreviated phonetic characters, adapted from Chinese characters.
6 *Encountering Sorrow* – here a free Japanese translation of the original Chinese poem. The probable author, Ch'u Yüan, was a virtuous nobleman who wrote the work during his own political exile.
7 *The Pillow Book of Sei Shōnagon*, written between 986 and 1000 AD, was the diary and notebook of a Court lady-in-waiting.
8 Nangaku. One of the sects of Chu Hsi Confucianist teaching which was founded in Tosa in the sixteenth century.
9 Alternate residence. As a limit upon his power and as a way of showing his loyalty, a lord, with his family and his servants, was required by the Government to spend alternate years in Edo.
10 Being a feudal society, if the province grew too rich, it would become a potential threat to the power of the Edo Government.
11 The custom of 'junshi' or suicide, to follow one's master to

the grave, was forbidden in a decree of 1663.

12 Tani Tanzaburō, also called Shinzan, born in Tosa (1662–1718).

13 Yamazaki Ansai (1618–82). Initially he was a Zen monk in Tosa. Later, as a famous scholar and orator in Edo, he amalgamated Shinto and Confucianist thought and re-interpreted Chu Hsi.

14 It was most eccentric behaviour for a woman of this age not to shave her eyebrows and blacken her teeth, whether single or married.

15 Ono no Komachi – a famous poetess of the ninth century – said to be a rare beauty who wrote sensitive poems.

16 This poem was extant, in the original Chinese, until 1945.

17 Shibukawa (1639-1715).

18 Kitabatake Chikafusa (1292–1354). A courtier and scholar who served the emperor at one of two rival courts in Japan at that time. Chikafusa wrote *Jin-nō Shōtōki* in 1339, a history which vindicated his emperor's divine legitimacy, according to Shintoist belief.

19 By the old lunar calendar, 1 February was the start of spring, and the start of the New Year.

20 *Nihon Shoki*. The oldest history compiled by a Government – completed in 720 AD, it chronologically relates events from the Age of the Gods to the 41st ruler, Emperor Jito.

21 Princess Sen-hime (1597-1666). Granddaughter of the first Tokugawa Shōgun. After two marriages, she took many lovers.

22 *The Great Learning*: *Daigaku* by Chu Hsi.

23 Bateren. Derogatory term, from patre = father; Portugese Jesuit missionaries of the sixteenth century.

24 Ogata Sotetsu (1644–1722).

25 Bagworm. Chrysalis of a psychid moth.

26 Classical Chinese expression, meaning happiness and peace of mind.

27 Kerria japonica.

28 Odo-ware – Tosa pottery.

Clan Lords of Tosa

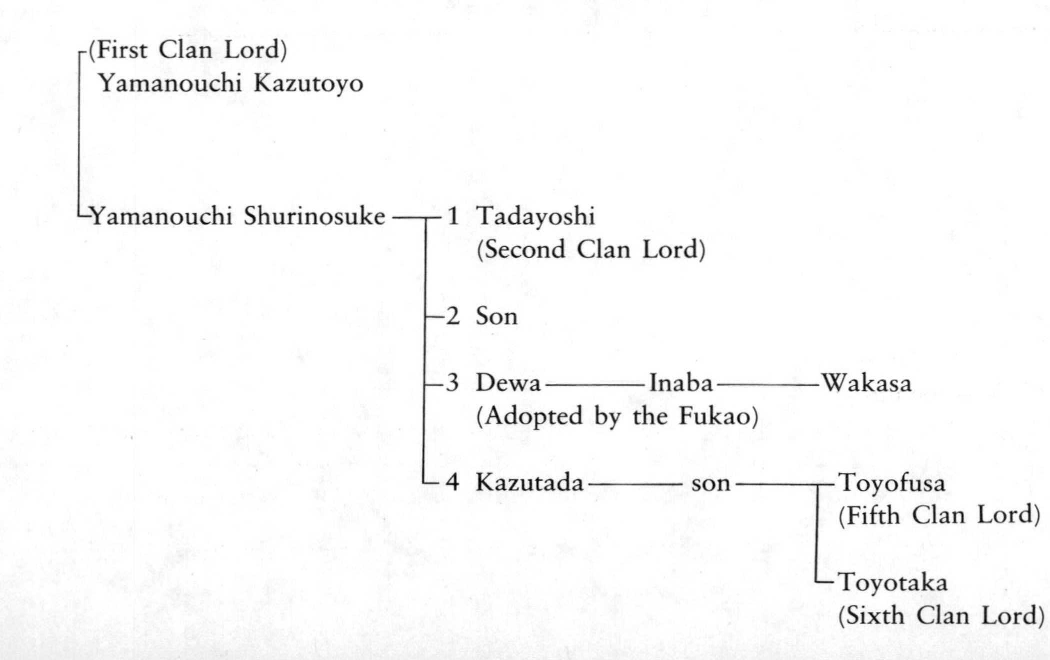

The Nonaka Family

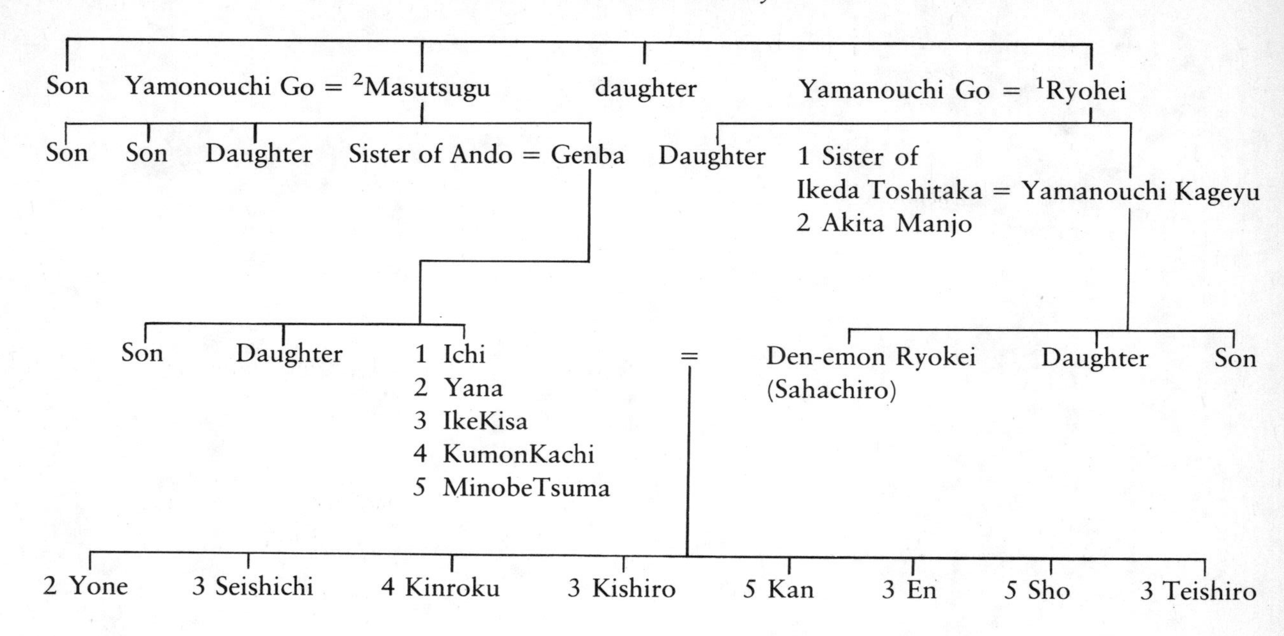